D0857121

3 1705 00213 1313

EYEWITNESS TO MURDER

BY

SOPHIE BELFORT

STATE LIBRARY OF OHIO
SEO Regional Library
Caldwell, Ohio 43724

DONALD I. FINE, INC.

NEW YORK

Copyright © 1992 by Sophie Belfort

All rights reserved, including the right of reproduction in whole or in part in any form. Published in the United States of America by Donald I. Fine, Inc. and in Canada by General Publishing Company Limited.

Library of Congress Cataloging-in-Publication Data

Belfort, Sophie.
Eyewitness to murder / by Sophie Belfort.
p.   cm.
ISBN 1-55611-292-0
I. Title.
PS3552.E474E97   1992
813'.54—dc20   91-58665
CIP

Manufactured in the United States of America

10 9 8 7 6 5 4 3 2 1

Designed by Irving Perkins Associates

This novel is a work of fiction. Names, characters, places and incidents are either the product of the author's imagination or are used fictitiously. Any resemblance to actual events, locales, organizations or persons, living or dead, is entirely coincidental and beyond the intent of either the author or publisher.

Revenge is nothing but the instinct of self-preservation, heightened by peril.

—EMILE DURKHEIM

CHAPTER

1

IGNATIUS HEALEY hurried up the red sandstone steps of the Arlington Street Church, the first Unitarian Church of Boston, "honored" in the last century, as the plaque beside the door reminded him, "by the ministry of William Ellery Channing." Healey paused at the top of the stairs and turned to look across Arlington Street at Channing's statue, set in a chaste classical niche at the entrance to the Public Garden: the minister stood gowned and ready to resume preaching. A foot, just visible beneath the hem of his robe, seemed poised to step down from its pedestal into the thick of some genteel fray. His right hand, now clutching the bronze folds of his gown, might at any moment be outflung in exhortation. "Think high thoughts," Channing would harangue tourists heading for the swan boats. "Free the slaves, educate the immigrants, enfranchise the ladies." Healey sneered. Reform, then and now, he believed, was crap. He'd have liked to dally in argument with that dully shining preacher, set him straight about a couple of things, but he was running late.

Exultant music met Healey as he entered the church and held him, briefly, in thrall:

Furious they assailed us
But Thy might availed us
And Thy word broke their swords
When our own strength failed us.

The mourners repeated the last two lines, should anyone have missed the point, *And Thy word broke their
swords / When our own strength failed us*, then continued:

Beneath the shelter of Thy wings
Thy saints have dwelt secure
Sufficient is Thine arm alone
And our defense is sure.

Caleb Tuttle's memorial service continued with the
combative hymns of the Reformation. The congregation,
savoring its victories, sang again. *The wicked oh press
ing cease then from dih stress ing/Sing prai ses to His
name He for gets not His own.* There was no place to sit,
every pew was full, the gallery packed, little room even
to stand at the back.

Ignatius Healey, small, plump, blond, pink-cheeked,
and needlessly rude in compensation for his cherubic appearance, jostled his way to an acceptable vantage point.
That achieved, he took a notebook from his breast pocket
and began jotting down the names of conspicuous mourners: upper-crust academic types, some Israelis he had met
before in not-very-amicable proceedings, a former director of the CIA. And, look at that, the Russian ambassador.
What more did anybody need to know about these people?
But was the German there? Yes, there he was, sitting with
a couple, they seemed to be a couple, whom Healey did
not recognize. He was there all right, but when had he
arrived? Too late, yes, almost certainly too late to have

seen Caleb Tuttle, who had said nothing about meeting with him. Too late to do anything but pay his last respects. God willing, Healey prayed.

A man sitting on the aisle, on the other side of the German, rose and walked up to the pulpit. He read an activist psalm, ". . . the Heavens belong to the Lord, but the earth He has given to the children of man," then returned to sit beside his wife, whose cheeks were wet with tears. Healey did recognize them. Limousine liberals. Hackneyed phrase, and decidedly wrong about these people who, Healey fully grasped, would never own or even rent a limousine; still the phrase was evocative and he used it from time to time in his syndicated column, *Ignatius Healey Speaks* because he liked alliteration. "Left-leaning liberationists," "supine so-called social Catholics." He longed to write *soi-disant*, but only Bill Buckley could get away with that. Nonetheless, to the best of his considerable ability Healey flailed liberals and, above all, "liberal" Catholics, cafeteria Catholics, gutless, all-but-apostate ecumenists, like that damned expiating Kraut.

The German was whispering something to the red-haired woman who sat beside him; she looked back over her shoulder in his direction. She was attractive, Healey thought, in a pale, classy way and there was nothing discourteous in her gaze. He tried and failed to catch her eye. Apparently she didn't recognize him as a celebrity. She spoke briefly to the German and then turned to the man on her other side, a very different type from the rosy-faced Hun. Dark, intense Mediterranean sort. Healey felt sure he knew which one she was sleeping with. He didn't have much luck with women himself. The Christian movement groupies believed in marriage, and the libertarians, by and large, did not like him.

Short as the watch that ends the night before the rising

sun. The final hymn. Well, not on his watch either. Not on Ignatius Healey's watch would this crowd persecute God-fearing men. He wished for the hundredth time that Father Paul had asked his advice before claiming sanctuary. The old man had panicked, as best Healey could make out, after a call from the State Department and driven himself—half blind though he was, his guardian angel must have been steering—to St. Anselm's, once a seminary, now a home for aged and convalescing priests in the Pennsylvania coal country. The hospice was set among slag-heaps and dust-covered clumps of mountain laurel, the bushes indistinguishable most of the year from other mounds of rubbish. To this insalubrious place, where only the strongest faith could hope for healing, Father Paul had fled; and it wasn't a bad choice. The diocese that supported St. Anselm's was sound, its bishop himself the faithful son of Polish immigrants. The cardinal, on the other hand, the cardinal whom that self-effacing bishop would surely obey, was capable of anything.

But now Caleb Tuttle, the only American who had been in the town of Zborodny in the summer of 1942, one of the very few people left in the world who had been there or admitted to having been there, was dead. There wasn't much argument about what had happened that August day and long into the night. The Germans had filmed everything, and five authenticated prints of their films survived: one with Wiesenthal in Vienna, two in Israel, and two recently rediscovered in Ukraine. Of these two, one was held by the Ministry of Justice in Kiev, and the other had been sent to Washington in support of the demand that Father Paul be extradited to stand trial for war crimes. The Ukrainian prints were particularly good: local collaborators had preserved them because they made plain that Slavs could participate as equals in the great endeavor to rid Europe of Jews.

The man some said was Father Paul had been energetic, demonically energetic—one might almost say possessed—during the hours of mass murder. Healey believed it to be a case of mistaken identity. His mentor was a man of fierce enthusiasms but, in his personal relations, remarkably gentle, a teacher who showed his students an almost feminine tenderness. Some of Paul's defenders acknowledged that he might, as a very young man, have witnessed, or even taken part in, terrible deeds. That was, in fact, the line one of the canon lawyers was proposing they take: Father Paul had found redemption in an encounter with absolute Evil. He'd been a Nazi for two, perhaps three, years and a servant of God for four decades. The soul's journey was mysterious, not, as the Puritans thought, a straight and narrow path, but unchartable. The civil lawyers Healey consulted thought that tack sounded risky: better to deny everything and insist on the presumption of innocence.

Healey had been simply afraid for the old man. He'd never questioned his innocence. That he'd taken for granted; he'd taken for granted also that nobody involved in the affair gave a damn about his guilt or his innocence. Everything Healey had done he'd done with the certainty that the old priest was being sacrificed, almost fifty years after the events, to some old and some new agendas. Healey had never imagined that anyone could truthfully swear to events that had happened so long ago, but habits of authority die hard. Tuttle's advice had been sought and taken throughout his adult life. He'd been an embodiment of the liberal establishment, so authoritative, so hegemonic that, Healey fancied, he'd never had occasion to raise his voice since the early days of the New Deal. That voice was silenced now, forever. Who would not give thanks?

Father Paul was soft-spoken himself in an English that had never become fluent or idiomatic. He'd arrived in

America in 1946 speaking not a word of English; he'd thought then of entering a contemplative order where he could meditate, he once told his protégé, in whatever language he chose. The native tongue of the alleged war criminal was, as it happened, one of the awkward points: the suspect came from a Ukrainian family and was said to have spoken a heavily accented and not wholly grammatical Polish. Father Paul had been born near Krakow in southern Poland, but his Polish was far from perfect, and Healey had written a column, carefully researched, about the possibility of forgetting one's mother tongue.

Nonetheless, Paul preached indefatigably on every occasion, public or private, at retreats and commencements, at the ordinations or weddings of his students, at the christenings of their children. The New World had appalled him. America was missionary territory, *in partibus infidelium*; in its wilderness he could not keep silent. The indifference with which American children accepted their schoolmates' heresies shocked him, as did the vapid hedonism of their parents. And that had been in the forties and fifties, Healey mused, before the Pill, before pot and crack and two-career families and gay pride. The past most of Healey's circle wanted to restore had seemed to Father Paul a place of utter desolation: there were no shrines beside American roads, only billboards and hamburger stands. For forty years, he'd sown the seed of unvarying Truth among this genial, tolerant people, and nowhere had the seedling taken deeper root than in the fecund soil of Ignatius Healey's adolescent soul.

Healey, whom Father Paul had taught to loathe compromise, would fight to the death for him. Yet even Healey wished his mentor could be a little clearer about his wartime experiences. Persecution and exile had fuddled him, one saw that. His memories of his boyhood before the war were sharp; he was precise too about the period in 1939, after the Germans had invaded from the west, when the Bolsheviks swept into eastern Poland. There had been decent Germans, he maintained, but no decent Reds. When the Germans had driven the Russians out, their soldiers protected the wayside shrines sacred to Our Lady.

He remembered countless details about the four shrines in his village. From the earliest spring, peasants set bowls of fresh flowers within the sturdy frames that sheltered the painted wooden statues. China flowers brought from as far away as Vienna would lie at Mary's feet year round; flowers twisted out of tissue paper also— "and, remember, *Ignatiku*," Father Paul said, using a diminutive form of his name, "that colored paper was rare and precious." Pious women would save scraps of cloth and sew them into roses or chrysanthemums; a woman might work for years to make a bouquet. Garlands of fresh or artificial flowers would be strung from the surrounding trees and fences, tendrils binding the shrine to the wood, connecting the earth with its mother. If a village had a generator, electric lights were strung also, not every day, but on holidays. It would be the Germans, often, who brought the first generator. Once, the bulbs had been lit from the battery of a young colonel's Mercedes. The wind had blown out the candles, but the lights had burned all night. Father Paul had told him this story many times; regrettably, chronological details were less clear, and the summers of the forties, Healey had found, impossible to reconstruct.

Healey lingered in the back of the church after the service, making sure he'd missed nobody of any importance. He had to write his column now and fax it to Washington, unless somebody at the hotel knew how to hook up his lap-top to a modem. Healey stepped out into the dappled May sunlight. William Ellery Channing's green visage shone in its ungarlanded grotto where no passerby had ever been moved to kneel. A heavy woman in a red tee-shirt was picketing Channing—or the Public Garden or something else of which she disapproved—holding a hand-lettered sign Healey could not read. Across the woman's huge sexless breasts her conviction that "PATRIARCHY SUCKS" was plainly stencilled; Channing appeared untroubled by her protest.

"Careful, Mr. Healey." The preacher's candid eye caught his. "Don't jump to conclusions," Channing seemed to warn him. "You're new in Boston, aren't you?"

CHAPTER

2

"**W**OLFI," Molly Rafferty said, "look at Healey's column. It's monstrous, enraging." She handed her houseguest the morning paper, folded to the op-ed page, and cut him a slice of hot soda bread. "I can't believe he had the gall to show up at the service."

Wolfgang Ritter shook his head with the deep sadness peculiar to good Germans. "Impious, really impious. Delicious, Molly," he added politely, nibbling the bread as he continued to read.

"Just that," she exclaimed. "Here, let me butter you another piece. Honey or marmelade?"

"Honey, please. This is fantastical. I had heard, but I had not imagined it would look like this, so like a missal." The initial letters of the column, *Ignatius Healey Speaks*, were set in Gothic letters, 𝕴𝕳𝕾. "One cannot but think, '*in hoc signo.*'"

"Healey's a brawler. He sees himself as a one-man Church Militant."

"It is blasphemous." Ritter was a sincerely pious man. "I suppose he cannot be prevented, in this country, from using the letters in such a way?"

"He's copyrighted the IHS logo in that typeface."

"Copyrighted it? God in heaven, but your right wing is odd."

"Heaven preserve them in their oddity," she said. "It keeps them marginal. Nick—" Nick Hannibal, Molly's fiancé, joined them at the breakfast table. Hannibal was, ordinarily, an early and sunnily cheerful breakfaster. He was late this morning because he'd gotten to bed at three after swapping shifts with another detective, who was having marital problems. "Nick, you will not believe Healey today." She took a carton of milk from the refrigerator. "There's coffee in the pot, and we'll have more hot milk in a minute or two."

"Molly's bread is very good," Wolfi said, passing the loaf and the paper. "Healey, on the other hand, is not so good."

"Read it aloud, would you?" Molly whisked the milk fiercely. "I want to hear it again."

" 'The Angel of Death has written *finis* to a sacrilegious vendetta. The death of the old partisan and fellow traveller Caleb Tuttle providentially closes a case human justice was powerless to resolve.' "

"Human justice was just about to get a crack at it." Molly was furious. She topped Nick's coffee with frothy milk and, looking over his shoulder, continued. " 'Tuttle had not been content, in his retirement, to cultivate his garden, his epicurean *potager*. Instead, he continued to sally forth from that ecologically correct bower to trouble a world he had long ceased to understand. But Caleb Tuttle has passed, at long last, from the City of Man into the realm of Divine Justice. His death comes as a sign to set aside sterile hatreds. It summons the living to abandon futile vengeance and confront instead the very real moral miasma in which our society festers today.' "

"Can one say that, to fester in a miasma?" Wolfgang Ritter asked, eager to improve his English.

"I wouldn't," Hannibal advised.

"When has Healey ever walked away from a 'sterile hatred'? He feeds on them." Molly took a sip of coffee and read on. " 'Let us get on with our spiritual lives, let us plunge with resolution and cleansing wrath into the swamp of pornography, promiscuity, sodomy, euthanasia, fetal tissue culturing . . .' *Tissue culturing.* Can you believe it? He's worried about what's going on in petri dishes and he believes there's some sort of divine statute of limitation on war crimes."

"One of the joys of breakfasting with Molly," Nick told their guest, "lies in watching her read Healey's column. It's like living with a particularly bigoted village atheist around 1850."

"1850?" Ritter was, like Molly Rafferty, a historian and he questioned the date. "Earlier, I would say."

"Earlier in the Rhineland, Wolfi," Molly said. "1850's about right for southern Italy."

"So, how will you be married?" His question was not an impertinence; it followed naturally and Molly and Nick were happy to discuss the problem with him. Few of their other friends understood the difficulty.

"We haven't decided," Molly said. "We could have a civil ceremony, of course, though they're very charmless. There is one way that wouldn't be charmless, to be married by the City Solicitor in Newnham City Hall. The council chambers are beautiful, grey and white and taupe, with splendid Federal woodwork."

"Tocquevillian." Wolfi recognized the appeal.

"Yes, but, a political risk for our friend, the City Solicitor," Nick explained. Their friend planned to run soon for mayor of Newnham. It was acceptable for him, as a justice of the peace, to marry Protestants or mixed couples, but a blue-collar electorate would not approve his marrying two apparent Catholics. Catholics were married by priests, or ought to be.

"My parents are up for anything," Molly said, "but they think I'm being pigheaded. And Nick's mother, who's wonderful, assumes we'll be married in Queen of Heaven, of which she's been a pillar all her married life."

"It will be this summer?" Wolfi wanted to make sure.

"Yes," Nick said. The details did not much concern him, but he liked Molly's vehemence. She was as fervent in her own way as his mother was in hers.

"Late in July, so we can go away during Nick's vacation in August and be back before the fall term starts at Scattergood."

"If you're free in June, you really should come to Krakow." Ritter was one of the organizers of a scholarly conference on the Reformation and Counter-Reformation in Eastern Europe. "We need people who know about Western heresies. I could fit you into any number of panels."

"I've never been farther east than Vienna," Molly said. "I'm very tempted."

"It would be good if you could come." Everyone wanted to visit Eastern Europe these days, and Ritter knew that many of the academics who'd accepted his invitation would do little more than put in an appearance and read a chapter of their current project. The rest of the time they'd be sight-seeing. "Many of the most, I think you say, stuffy people will be there. I wish you would come too."

"How far is Krakow from the place where Tuttle witnessed the killings?" Nick asked.

"Zborodny? Not far. I will be going there myself." Ritter served as lay advisor to a group of German bishops who had recommended a thorough review of the ecclesiastical aspects of Nazi rule in Eastern Europe. It was in this capacity that he had come to America to interview Caleb Tuttle.

"Isn't it in Ukraine now?" Molly asked.

"Yes, but during the war it was administered as part of German-occupied Poland. The eastern Ukraine was under direct military rule and those records were lost in the retreat. The *Reichscommissariat* in Krakow had a little more time to ship its records home. That's why we know as much as we do about Zborodny."

"And the films." Few of Ritter's contemporaries, Molly knew, would say "German-occupied," rather than "Nazi-occupied."

"Yes. In southern Poland the occupying forces relied on the sort of people who preserved them. Some Poles were willing to collaborate, but they were not so useful because most of the pro-German peasants spoke Ukrainian."

"The Russians had treated the Ukrainians brutally." Molly felt this fact explained more than it excused.

Ritter acknowledged her point with the same reservations. "Even so . . ."

"How different are the languages?" Nick asked. "Can people understand each other?"

"They are related," he explained, "but they are written with different alphabets. Hard as the devil, both of them. I've been studying Polish."

Characteristically, Molly thought.

"They decline everything, nouns, pronouns, proper names, even numbers, in six cases."

"You mean they don't have a real language yet?" Nick regarded the progression from Latin to Italian as a natural one.

"Not a vernacular," Ritter said. "People are very proud of speaking correctly, if they do. And it emphasizes class differences, of course. Forty years of communism did nothing to equalize grammar."

"It really does sound like an interesting place." Molly began to wonder if she could spare the time.

"It would interest you, Molly," he persisted. "The manners are not like the West. Hand-kissing, bowing, many things survive that would mark a Frenchman or an Italian as a monarchist—"

"Or worse," Nick said.

"Or worse," Ritter agreed. It was tactful of Molly's man to acknowledge that every country had skeletons in its political closet. "All kinds of old-regime practices continue. I think because they associate egalitarian ways with the Russians."

"Rather than with some indigenous revolution," Molly suggested. "Tuttle always said the rural areas were virtually feudal before the war."

"Just so. Deference, obedience, these are hard habits to break." Ritter inhaled and exhaled sharply, a breath too emphatic to be a sigh and expressing even deeper regret. "It is unfortunate Caleb Tuttle did not live to review those films. An eyewitness and so trustworthy. I regret it more than I can say." He rose from the table. "Breakfast was very good, Molly. Thank you."

"You ought to go to Krakow, babe," Nick said, after Wolfi had gone to finish packing. Ritter was returning to Cologne that night, but he planned to spend the day with Molly at Scattergood College, the small, selective women's college where she taught.

"I'd like to . . . Wolfi seems to want me to come."

"He's desperate to have you there. You can't let the poor guy go by himself."

"He's agonizingly good," Molly said, picking up the newspaper as she began to clear the breakfast table. "It's obscene the way Healey is crowing over Tuttle's death. 'The Angel of Death has written *finis*.' Get the phone, would you?"

"The Angel of Death had some help," Nick said, as he hung up the phone a few minutes later. "Caleb Tuttle was poisoned."

"No." Molly set down the bread very deliberately. "Poisoned? How is that possible?" Caleb Tuttle's death had saddened her, but she'd been comforted by the ease and seemliness of his dying, at a venerable age, in his sleep and at home. Her old teacher's death had been as civilized, as enviable as his life. "How do you know? You never told me there'd been an autopsy."

"There wasn't. He left his body to science."

"As, of course, he would."

"As someone did not know him well enough to anticipate that he would," Nick said. "A couple of bright medical students didn't like the look of his liver. They weren't sure, but they thought it worth pursuing. Their anatomy professor called Riordan in Homicide and Riordan called me."

"Do you know what it was?"

"Barium salt in some medium immiscible in oil, possibly in salad dressing."

"The old partisan," Molly said, "fought the good fight all his life, survived underground for years, and they finally got him in the house where he was born. Damn them."

"Them?" Nick asked, amused by her zeal and her certainty.

"No," she acknowledged. "I don't know that his death had anything to do with his politics. I don't know that he was murdered before he could identify a reactionary writer's mentor as a war criminal. But every decent person who ever met him loved and revered him. Dear God, wait till Wolfi hears this."

CHAPTER

$$\boxed{3}$$

THE TUTTLE House, a Federal mansion of some historic interest, was set back from the street, its lawn and ample garden incongruously draped with yellow plastic tape marking a police line to be crossed by authorized persons only. Weathered, but well kept, the house shone with a patina of wealth amassed and civic duty discharged. New England antiquarians recognized it as the most comfortable stop on the Underground Railroad: fugitive slaves had been accommodated in its wine cellar, from which a tunnel led to the banks of the Charles River. Lt. Nick Hannibal, pausing on the brick front walk, noted above its open door an American eagle, carved with singular vigor, grasping a leafy olive branch and a clutch of workmanlike arrows. A flag, at half-mast, hung motionless in the still air.

Caleb Tuttle's housekeeper stood in the doorway with a uniformed officer. They were expecting him. The two lower floors of the house had been unoccupied after Tuttle's death—the housekeeper was staying with relatives—and then sealed after toxic residues were discovered a week later in the tissues of his liver. Hannibal had

20

ordered routine measures for a crime scene with little hope that any evidence would survive.

Tuttle had been found dead late on a Friday morning: someone in the house called 911; an ambulance and two cruisers, responding to a "possible sudden death," got there at noon. The EMTs were pretty sure nothing could be done for Tuttle and took him, after minimal treatment at the scene, to the nearest hospital, where time of death was established as about ten hours earlier. The cause of death, "heart failure," had since been revised, but pathologists thought nothing in the poison's action would affect the initial clinical estimate of time of death, an hour or so after midnight the previous night. The fatal substance, depending on the dosage and possibly also on reactions with prescription drugs, might have been ingested as much as forty-eight hours before, maybe earlier if given in a time-release form. The lab hadn't gotten the chemistry completely sorted out. It was possible that a reaction between patent and prescription drugs, rather than deliberate poisoning, had killed Tuttle. That was not likely but it hadn't been completely ruled out. Preliminary inquiries held suicide unlikely also, even though death seemed to have been painless, and the deceased was known to be a determined rationalist. Hannibal believed he was dealing with murder.

The housekeeper, an elderly woman dressed in a crisp black cotton dress, extended her hand to him and shook his firmly. "I am Mrs. Alexander," she said. "You wanted to talk with me."

"Yes, please." Hannibal asked the policeman to remain at the door and followed her into a large sitting room on the left of the central hall. He was impressed by the dignity of her bearing; she limped slightly and held her head and upper body erect. She appeared entirely at ease in the room, mistress of herself and, albeit in no proprietary way, of the household as well.

"It's a beautiful room," Hannibal said, as if to acknowledge her share in it. Long windows reached almost to the shining floor, a few panes held violet glass, old as the house itself and prized now for its flaws. The furnishings, too, were fine, worn, and unapologetic. The Tuttles had been cosmopolitan for generations: inlaid chests, trophies of the China trade, stood next to Shaker chairs on Turkish rugs. Naive seascapes, swelling with bottle green waves and salmon pink clouds, hung on faded walls. High thinking, Nick thought, and not very plain living. New England's silvery prime.

"Many friends met here," Mrs. Alexander said. "Caleb Tuttle had many friends." She was resigned, Nick sensed, but deeply troubled by his death.

"I've heard only good things about him."

"Good, yes. Remarkable. He was a remarkable man."

"I'm sorry."

She bowed her head for a moment, then looked up. "What can I tell you? He was busy until the last day. He never stopped working and people came almost every day to see him."

"But he'd had a heart attack? He rested and paced himself?"

She nodded. "He lived," she paused. She spoke with a faint accent; Molly had told him she was an Eastern European who'd been with Tuttle since the war. She seemed to hesitate, though, not because an English word escaped her but because she took care to use the right one. "With wisdom, good sense, except . . ." There followed a longer pause.

"Except for what?"

"He was too trusting. An American," she said, as if that said it all.

Hannibal would encourage her to expand on that important point later. First he wanted to get the events straight. "You weren't here when he died?"

She shook her head. "I had left on Thursday for the weekend."

Nick was interested chiefly in events beginning Wednesday morning, but that wasn't public knowledge. Instead, he inquired about the preceding week: visitors, activities, meals eaten out and at home. There were questions, too, about Caleb Tuttle's health.

He knew Tuttle'd suffered two previous heart attacks. A respected Boston cardiologist had provided a list of drugs he'd sparingly prescribed. After the first attack, a serious one in Tuttle's late sixties, a careful routine of diet and exercise kept him in good condition until another, milder attack four years before, when Tuttle was 79. His age prompted doctors to propose more aggressive treatment: exercise had been scaled back and Tuttle had taken an anticoagulant daily. He kept on hand pills to be taken in the event of certain kinds of chest pains, and he had antihistamines for allergies that had troubled him from boyhood. A passionate gardener, he would, in no season, deny himself the pleasure of his plants. He'd never used pain medication or sleeping pills.

Mrs. Alexander's account of his medicines coincided in every detail with the doctor's report. "He took the anticoagulant after breakfast," she added, "because it was not to be taken on an empty stomach."

"Do you remember what he had for breakfast on Wednesday?"

"I remember clearly," she said. "He ate more for breakfast than he usually did. Oatmeal, stewed apricots, coffee, and some black bread toast with thick honey, no butter. He wanted to be out all day in the garden."

"So, you didn't see him at lunchtime?"

"I saw him briefly. I was busy preparing dinner. He helped himself to some of the soup we were having that night. It was a favorite of his, a sour soup, made from sorrel and chard, and some apple compote and black bread."

"And dinner?" Hannibal asked. "You served it?"

"I cooked it. Students came in to serve and clean up when he had a large party. There were twelve guests that night." She described an elaborate meal. Several of the courses included a possible medium for the poison, but every dish had been served to a tableful of guests.

"Mrs. Alexander, I think you told the police last week you left early for the weekend. When was that? Thursday morning?"

She nodded. "I made sure he was all right before I left."

"Made sure?" Her English was precise. She must mean just that. "Were you concerned about him?"

"I accuse no one, Lieutenant, but I was worried. That night, the night before, he was entertaining a group of Ukrainians. He was always in touch with dissidents, and now many of them are in power. They came to ask his advice about writing a democratic constitution, or so they said."

"He must have been happy to help."

"He was happy," she said, "He was not naive, but he had hopes." She sounded as if she did not share them. "The worst apparatchiks are saying now that in their hearts they were never communists," she continued. "They are lying. They're simply opportunists."

Nick smiled. "Even Americans can recognize that."

"But others"—she rose from her chair awkwardly; the injury that accounted for her limp seemed to make it difficult for her to change positions—"Others," she said, walking to the windows that looked out onto the garden, "others are telling the truth." She spoke softly and bitterly. "The truth."

Nick went over to her. It was some minutes before she spoke again. "They were Nazis, they were always fascists.

They'd been with the Germans but they'd managed to foul their tracks. We heard how people came back, claiming they'd been prisoners, claiming they'd fought with the Red Army . . ." She was not close to tears. Her fury did not permit such weakness, but she leaned against the window, spent, when the surge of anger passed.

"Tell me," he said, leading her back to a sofa where she could sit next to him. "Tell me about yourself."

CHAPTER

4

"MY MAIDEN name was Olia Petroskaya," she began in the patient monotone used by persons who rarely speak about themselves save in response to official questions. "I was born in 1922 in a part of Galicia that became Polish after the First World War. My parents were poor farmers so the political changes meant little to us. When I was sixteen I got married—Alexander is the English form of my husband's name—and went to live with him on the estate where he worked."

"Did you work too, after your marriage?"

"I was very soon pregnant, but I helped in the kitchen. We lived in a small cottage on the estate. The family was good to us, even when things became difficult for them. The mistress was sick in the spring of 1939, and her daughter came home to take care of her. Strange as it seems to remember it now, it was a beautiful summer." Her voice grew warmer. She was telling a story, not complying with a demand for information. "We'd never seen so many currants and raspberries. We made jam, the young mistress and I, for weeks. She was studying medicine at the university and she taught me to sterilize the

26

jars very carefully. She said trouble was coming and the jam would have to last us a long time."

"You had a baby by that time?" Nick wondered how she'd managed with an infant during the fighting and the occupation.

"The child was stillborn."

"I'm sorry." Perhaps her husband had been killed in the war too, and she'd been alone in the world.

"Zosha, the daughter, was encouraging me to leave my husband." That emancipated advice cut short his musing, and he listened closely as Olia Alexander fixed her eyes on the brown husks of lilac blossoms pressing against the tinted windowpanes and gave him the reasons that the educated girl had urged upon her.

Men should not beat their wives, and her husband regularly beat her. Customarily, he beat her on Saturday nights, when he came home drunk from the village. Pan Josef, the master, would lock him in the stable and he'd scream and plead to be let out. If only he were set free, he promised, he would not hurt his wife. Every week, the master's son would beg his father to take pity on him and every week his father would refuse. The boy was insistent and idealistic. He thought his father underestimated the peasantry; many times she'd heard them arguing, the father shouting, "They are not like us." One night she'd unlocked the door for her husband herself, and the master had found her unconscious. After that Pan Josef hid the key to the stable.

The rural areas were virtually feudal before the war, Molly had said. So they seemed to have been, and Pan Josef had the right idea: decent men protected women who could not protect themselves. Maybe that was paternalistic, but Nick believed it. And this woman's husband hadn't had the balls to attack another man; he'd simply howled to be set free so he could beat her again.

"When my baby was born dead," she continued, her voice cold and toneless as it had been when she began, "he beat me even when he was sober." A barren woman was apparently no use to him, and he made little protest when the family let her sleep in the big house. "But they were a Jewish family," she said, "and in time my husband had his revenge."

That frightful story rang true. Nick hadn't realized there'd been Jewish landowners in that part of the world—Molly would know about the fluctuating levels of religious toleration—but he'd heard of Italian partisans who'd found the peasantry sympathetic with most of their program, but wedded, so to speak, to wife-beating. That was a custom men cherished—and the fascists, however unreasonable they might be about taxes and conscription, never meddled with it.

"The Germans promised him the house and land." She spoke matter-of-factly and Nick imagined these transactions had been routine. "They slaughtered the family and most of the other servants. I hid the daughter, Zosha, in my parents' house."

"Your parents were brave people."

"Even so, we did not stay with them long. We made our way to a group of partisans. There was an American with them." Her fine thin lips parted in a smile. "When Zosha found out his name was Caleb, she laughed. Caleb was a spy in the Bible, too. Moses sends him as a scout into the Promised Land. Zosha said Caleb had come to the wrong place."

Tuttle had kept a gold ring with some souvenirs of the war in his office safe at Marvell College. Nick had seen it in the course of an earlier investigation and he sensed he was about to learn whose ring it was. "And they became good friends?"

"They were lovers. She promised to marry him after the war."

"What happened?"

"My husband killed her. He'd been looking for her, I think. He expected the Germans to win and make good their promises to him, but he did not like to take chances and he led the raid on our camp. They killed others but Zosha was the one they came for. I was shot in the hip and nobody bothered to finish me off."

"Tuttle survived also?"

"He was away, at Zborodny. People were being rounded up and kept there, so we knew something was about to happen. He went to see what he could do. Nothing, as it turned out."

Nick thought about that: to witness death on an almost unimaginable scale, helpless to prevent it, and then to find dead the woman you might have saved.

"When Caleb got back, he stalked and killed her killers."

"Good."

She'd never told an American this story and Nick's response surprised and pleased her. "Caleb brought me back to America with him after the victory. My husband's family blamed me and his brothers didn't want me alive to claim the land. They'd been collaborators, now they were landlords. We got word the Russians killed them all. I hope they did."

And people say Sicily's violent, he thought. "I hope you've found some peace here."

"I have been very happy here. The past was very distant . . ."

"Until Ukrainian dissidents were free to travel?"

"You understand." She liked Hannibal. He was quick and highly sympathetic. "Caleb just laughed. He said men don't choose their fathers."

"You're going too fast," he said.

"On the Wednesday night, when the constitution writers came to dinner, I recognized one of them. Not the man himself, a generation younger, but a man who looked like a man who'd been a collaborator." Olia Alexander said she'd caught a glimpse of him through the pantry hatch as she handed out dishes to the students who were serving. She'd told Tuttle when he came into the kitchen after dinner, and he'd dismissed her fears. "I was afraid," she continued. "This man ate his soup just the way his father did, greedily, sloppily. Most of these dissidents, Lieutenant"—she laid a hand on his sleeve and bent forward earnestly—"most are educated men and women, refined. This man is not of bourgeois family. And," she said, appearing to find this conclusive, "his name was not the same as his father's."

"It could be a chance resemblance." Nick felt obliged to point this out.

"He had a fat face with a mole between his eyes and one on his chin, just like the other. If the name had been the same," she explained, "I would not have been so worried. He was an obscure villain, not so famous that a son needed to change his name. But I believe the whole group flew to Washington after they left this house. And Caleb was fine the next morning."

"How well did he know the others in the group?"

"He'd corresponded with several of them for years. He'd seen some of them earlier this spring when he was travelling in Eastern Europe. He trusted them."

"This obscure villain," Nick asked, "has he any connection with the man the Ukrainians want to extradite?"

"None that I know of. He was a much smaller fish. Brutal, but humble, not given much responsibility. He seems a minor player in this generation too," she added wryly.

"Did you ever see the man they want to put on trial?"

"I don't think so. Caleb described him to me, after Zborodny and again this spring. He sounded like a hundred others. I can't be sure I ever knew him."

"And the last question for now, ma'am. Did you actually see Caleb Tuttle before you left the house on Thursday morning?"

"Yes. I tapped on his door and he asked me to take the cat out. The cat spends the night in the bedroom and he's very demanding, sometimes, in the morning, that people pay attention to him. Caleb wished me a pleasant weekend and said he'd go back to sleep for an hour or so."

"If it's no trouble I'd like to see the bedroom."

"None at all. I can manage the stairs." She preceded him up the central spiral staircase, using the banister to lift herself from step to step. The master bedroom overlooked the garden at the back of the house; an open book had been left on the window seat and the smell of blossoming fruit trees filled the room. A big grey-and-white cat lay disconsolate in the middle of a double bed. The cat looked up as they entered and then turned away, curling its body into a tighter ball. Olia Alexander spoke soothingly to it and stroked its furry back.

"Who fed the cat, this past week?"

She explained that a family lived upstairs. They paid no rent in exchange for some chores. "The young man's a divinity student. He's been very reliable, though his wife's . . ." This time no English word came to her. "You'll want to see for yourself."

CHAPTER

$$\boxed{5}$$

A CHILD WAS wailing as Nick Hannibal climbed the back stairs to the top-floor apartment. It seemed to be crying, not in pain, but plaintively, in persistent, untended distress. A young woman with a thin face and bad skin answered the door. "Just a minute," she said. "I feel like shit. I'm pregnant again," she added unnecessarily; her blue denim workshirt bulged over tight jeans. "You might as well come in." She glanced around the living room and seemed to dismiss the thought of tidying it for the visitor.

Nick identified himself and asked if he should come back later.

"No time's likely to be any better for about five years," she said. She followed the detective's glance to the crying child, suspended listlessly in a jumping seat hung in a doorway. "There's another one napping," she said. "Great planning, huh?"

Nick found it surprising. This was the wife, presumably, of a *Protestant* divinity student. Molly, a lapsed Catholic, viewed contraception as she viewed votes for women, an incomparably precious victory over the forces of reaction. They'd have children, they hoped, but not like this.

"So, what do you want to know?" she asked after he'd told her something of his investigation. She seemed not to notice the child who was reaching out to her.

"Was it you or your husband who found Caleb Tuttle dead?"

"Neither of us. It was Jimmy and he called the cops."

Jimmy, Nick learned, helped Caleb Tuttle in the garden. He did not work daily, generally a couple days each week. He was not there now, but she had a number for him. He'd told her husband—whose name was William Flood; she was Daphne Robbins and used her maiden name for reasons that escaped Nick—that Tuttle usually left a check for him. He'd finished early and gone to find the boss to be paid before the weekend. Jimmy'd started working there that spring. Yes, she did know where he came from. Her husband had found him when he was doing his prison chaplaincy internship. Divinity school had a lot of projects like that and they all took a lot of time. He was off each semester with runaways or addicts or Brazilian pentecostals, some new and fascinating bunch of needy brothers and sisters. He got Jimmy this job to make him eligible for a work-release program, and Tuttle took an interest in him too. She could see them together from her kitchen window. They talked a lot while Jimmy was working in the garden. "Sometimes," she added, "he stopped up here for a beer after work."

"He owed a lot to your husband." It would be tough for her, with her husband away so much, to share him with the unfortunate at home too.

Daphne Robbins completely misunderstood. "You mean I shouldn't invite Jimmy up here? You think I fuck him when hubby's away?"

Nick was flabbergasted. Somebody, clearly, had slept with this dismal woman, but what, apart from a sense of obligation, would lead a man to do it?

"I didn't mean to suggest. I, please . . ." He was seldom speechless.

"Sorry. That old witch Olga, Olia, whatever, said some things to me about him. He is kinda cute. She tell you about her nephew?"

Olia Alexander had said nothing about a nephew, but Daphne told him a great deal. Mrs. Alexander had hurried away the Thursday morning before Caleb Tuttle died because her niece had called her. The niece's son, her great-nephew, was a spoiled suburban kid. The niece's husband had done well; he was a roofer or something and they lived out in Hawthorne, a rural town without a lot of class where people lived comfortably with satellite dishes and pick-up trucks. The kid was constantly in trouble. This time the police were looking for him in connection with some racist graffiti. It was a great source of shame and sorrow, Daphne explained maliciously. The kid was mixed up with a neo-Nazi gang. He'd been missing for days; that's why Mrs. Alexander stayed away so long. She was comforting her niece.

"Has the boy ever been here?"

"Yeah," she said. "He was here one day the week Caleb died. Old Olia brought the kid to the great man every now and then, so he could reason with him. There was a lot of shouting. I don't think reason prevailed."

"Where are you from, Ms. Robbins?" Nick asked.

"Greenwich, Connecticut, and Bennington College," she said. "Can't you see I'm nuts about spontaneity?"

He'd been wondering when she'd say she didn't like cops, or possibly "pigs" and why she hadn't said it before now.

"Would you mind coming down to Tuttle's kitchen with me?" he said. "I'll carry the baby, if you don't want to leave her."

She went in to check her other child—it was still sleeping and too young to get out of its crib—and followed him, heavily, downstairs.

"Mrs. Alexander said that the kitchen was clean when she got back," Nick told her. "Did you help Tuttle on Thursday?"

"Nope, all I did was feed the damn cat on Friday morning when I heard it meowing. It can't need food. It's fat as a badger already. I fed it to shut it up. I thought Caleb was sleeping late."

"Mrs. Alexander said everything in the dishwasher was clean. Would he have turned it on himself on Thursday night?"

"I guess he knew how."

She saw nothing out of place in the kitchen, but, she said, she wasn't interested in kitchens and wasn't likely to notice much about them; Nick judged that to be true. She could not remember or would not say what Tuttle had done on Thursday. Jimmy had been there. She'd gone out for a doctor's appointment in the morning and had no idea if anyone came for lunch. She had no memory of Thursday evening either, except that the older child had a fever and her husband was saying grace at a homeless shelter. It sounded grim. Nick thanked her and looked forward to meeting her husband and Jimmy. The little girl began to whimper as he handed her back to her mother.

Mrs. Alexander, whom he sought out in the garden, was feeding bread to a great golden carp in an artificial pond. "In the summer we feed him slugs from the rosebushes," she said. "Caleb wouldn't use pesticides, and the fish thrive on slugs and beetles." She acknowledged all that Daphne Robbins had said about her niece's son. It was terrible, she said; American children have no conception how terrible. "I don't believe the boy could find Germany on a map of the world. And his parents have worked so hard."

"Could he have come here while you were with his parents in Hawthorne?"

"He could have been anywhere," she said. "But Caleb

would have called us if he'd seen him. He knew how worried we were."

"Ms. Robbins knows very little about Thursday," he said. "Can I go over the kitchen with you?"

Mrs. Alexander did not know if Tuttle had expected guests for Thursday lunch. There would have been left-overs from the dinner party, soup, cold meat, poached peaches. She couldn't be sure about quantities because the students who were serving had cleaned up and they'd been invited to help themselves. When she was going to be away for a day or two, she left washed lettuce wrapped in linen towels. That had been eaten and the towels hung up in the pantry.

"What about dressing?" Nick asked. "Would he have used a bottled salad dressing? There isn't any in the refrig-erator."

That suggestion appeared to shock her, but she cor-rected him politely. "He knew how to mix vinegar and oil himself. There's a little gadget that chops up herbs and mixes the liquids."

"Where do you keep it?"

She went immediately to a drawer on the left of the sink. "I put it back," she said. "I emptied the dishwasher when I came in on Saturday, the day after he died. I wanted to put the house in order. I think he must have gone out for dinner on Thursday night, or perhaps he was already feeling sick and went to bed without eating."

"You mean the dishwasher was clean but not full?"

"Yes, it was only half-full and the things inside looked clean. That surprised me because Caleb wouldn't have run the machine unless it was full. I switched it on again myself because I couldn't tell whether the plates had just been rinsed or actually washed. I wasn't thinking about evidence."

"No reason you should have been."

"I stripped his bed and did some laundry. I knew he wanted his clothes to go to charity. When I'd finished the laundry, I unloaded the dishwasher."

"Can you remember if there were enough plates and cups or whatever in the dishwasher for more than one person's meals?"

She couldn't remember and Nick urged her to try and visualize opening the machine and unloading it.

"I really cannot." She seemed to be struggling. "There must have been too much to do by hand. I'm frugal myself, so I must have thought it made sense to use the machine, but I was in a hurry to put the house in order." There was going to be a reception after the memorial service, she explained, and she thought at that time it would be at home. Later, they decided on his club because it was closer to the church.

"So he could have eaten a meal with another person?"

"I think so. Yes, a light meal."

"And after you put things in order on Saturday, what did you do?"

"I went back to my niece's house."

"Has her son come home?"

"His parents are really frightened this time," she told him. "He's never been away this long, almost three weeks. And he's been in so much trouble, the local police in Hawthorne don't treat him like a missing child, or a runaway. They're thankful he's out of their jurisdiction. I can't say I blame them."

"How old is he?"

"Eighteen."

"Maybe it's time for the world to teach him things he's got to learn." This family had, as the saying goes, suffered enough. Nick hoped the boy was alive and innocent of major felonies.

"Do you want him found?"

"Of course."

Hannibal took a teak salad bowl back to headquarters with him. It was unvarnished, wiped clean, the house-keeper said, and never washed with detergent. Possibly it had absorbed some salad oil and whatever was dissolved in it. He took back with him also two bottles of vinegar, white wine and balsamic, and several bottles of oil: corn, peanut, safflower, and toasted sesame oil; rich green extra-virgin olive oil; and a small tin of French walnut oil.

WILLIAM FLOOD, divinity student and husband of Daphne Robbins, called Hannibal late in the afternoon and offered to meet him in Boston. It was hard to have an adult conversation, he said, in a room full of children. Flood said Jimmy was doing very well on work release. He'd been doing time for a series of burglaries, never convicted of anything involving a weapon, not a vicious criminal. Caleb Tuttle had been pleased to help him and thought he had the makings of a gardener, if only he could make him a little more organic. Jimmy liked to spray things. He'd been incredulous when Tuttle told him you had to wash nasturtium leaves with soap and water to kill the aphids.

Flood admitted that his sorrow over Tuttle's passing was mixed with worry about their apartment. He wasn't sure who got the house; there were no surviving relatives. The Society for the Preservation of New England Antiquities was said to be interested and he thought his family might not be their ideal tenants. Nick couldn't tell him how long probate would take and did little to set his mind at rest. For the short term, however, his family could stay in the house. There was no direct access from their apartment into the floors where Tuttle lived except through the kitchen door off the back hall, and that door, as well as the cellar, had been sealed.

"I think Jimmy's father was a policeman," Flood said as he left Nick's office. "His father had some sort of blighted career. On the take, or something. I'm sure," he added, wishing to give no offense, "lapses like that are much rarer now."

CHAPTER

6

"THE UKRAINIANS want just one thing, Your Eminence," Ignatius Healey said, pitching his tone between contempt and condemnation. He meant to convey that the Ukrainians' depravity, shocking to persons less worldly than himself, merely confirmed his own wide experience.

"Then they're exceptional folk," the cardinal said mildly. "Most people want a lot of different things." John, Cardinal Hollihan, met with almost anyone who asked to see him, but he was notoriously impatient with pomp and with certain points of view. This afternoon he wore waders and glanced every few minutes out the window of his study: he'd promised to take a group of children fishing that afternoon, and he wanted to get them to the lake while a few hours of light remained.

"I mean in connection with this absurd persecution."

"Prosecution," the cardinal corrected, opening his tackle basket.

"Hard currency." Healey did not contest the point but pressed on. "That's what this is about, Your Eminence, hard currency." He paused, eager to elaborate.

"You mean they think that the Jews control the banks

and that they'll get no foreign loans, not even from the Germans, without a convincing show of contrition?"

That was exactly what Healey meant, but he'd hoped his insight would scandalize the cardinal.

"So what?" Cardinal Hollihan bent over a toolbox full of flies, transferring a careful selection to his tackle basket. He hit a button on his speakerphone. "Timmy, did you pick up the worms?" Satisfied with the answer, he explained: "A seminarian is helping me with the fresh-air kids."

"Your Eminence." Healey's tone was not respectful.

"I've been listening, Mr. Healey. The Ukrainians' motives are not pure. Well, tell me whose are? If they're as bigoted as you think they are, the trial may do them some good. Timmy"—he turned to his speakerphone again— "Don't forget the marshmallows. They're fine for bait if children are squeamish about worms, and we can toast the leftovers."

"A priest is about to be martyred, and you're going fishing. You, a prince of the Church, are going fishing."

Cardinal Hollihan closed the toolbox and seated himself in the tall leather-backed chair behind his desk. "And princes dispense justice, or they used to. A man in holy orders, a man subject to my authority, is accused of revolting crimes. What do you think I should do?" He was a fair-minded man, but peppery. He sat quietly for a few minutes. He had been ill and his face was gaunt, his skin pale and paper-thin over sharp cheekbones. Scant white hair bore no trace of the color that flamed above his altar boy's surplice when he'd first served mass. Only his tufted eyebrows, bristling above his sharp eyes, kept a tinge of foxlike red.

The cardinals elevated by Roncalli, Healey thought, that deplorable crowd-pleaser of a pope, John XXIII, were faltering, their days almost palpably numbered.

"What's the right response to a lawful request for extradition?" Hollihan challenged him. "What would you do in my place?"

"A priest has claimed sanctuary."

"American law doesn't recognize sanctuary."

"The Church should insist upon it." Healey spoke sententiously, but he was pleading with the cardinal.

"Don't be a fool, Healey. We've got a hundred religions. They can't all be above the law. We've got people in trailer camps worshipping rattlesnakes. White supremacists quoting the Bible. Polygamists shooting truant officers. This is America, not the Middle Ages."

"These unhappy facts are ephemeral. They have nothing to do with the truths of the Church."

"You remind me of some of my brothers-in-Christ, Healey." The cardinal reminisced and Healey bobbed his head, reverentially, at each familiar name. "And that one," Hollihan concluded, "never met a fascist he didn't like."

Healey was appalled. The old man was worse than the worst stories told about him. More than cantankerous—deranged. His mind was going.

"You must defend sanctuary." That seemed simple enough.

"You've heard of the First Amendment."

"Yes, but I know something about politics too. I've been assured at the highest levels, the very highest levels . . ."

The cardinal nodded impatiently. "I know."

"They won't use force to remove a priest from church grounds. Not in an election year."

"So they tell me. If I say Paul's too sick to travel, they'll leave it at that."

Healey, greatly relieved, sat down, although the cardinal had not, up till then, invited him to be seated. He settled himself comfortably in an armchair and unbuttoned his double-breasted blazer. "Then there's no problem. It doesn't raise any constitutional issues."

"Or," Hollihan said, ignoring him, "I can order Paul to surrender himself."

"For what possible reason?" Healey was too shocked to rise. He slumped deeper into the chair. "On what conceivable grounds?"

"He may be guilty. I can't judge that myself."

Before Healey could fix upon the proper response to this infamy—whether to stalk out in silence, shriek his outrage, or seize the speakerphone and summon help from Rome, Boston, and Washington—Cardinal Hollihan spoke again. "I'd counted on Caleb Tuttle's advice. I hear, unofficially, there's a suspect in his murder."

"Two suspects. Two equally unsavory young men."

"Working together?" the cardinal asked and then raised his hand for silence. Hard upon a tap on the door, a small pigtailed girl dashed into the room. "Julia?"

"We're ready, papa John," she said. "Aren't you coming?"

"In a minute, sweetheart. Do you want to take the tackle basket down to the van?" He helped her adjust the strap over her shoulder. "It's not too heavy?"

She shook her head and left, bearing the basket proudly. The archdiocese ran a fresh-air camp on the farm that served as the cardinal's summer residence, and children came and went freely at the fieldstone farmhouse. The cardinal's study had once been the parlor, a low-ceilinged room with doors leading to a front porch covered with honeysuckle.

"The children are waiting," Hollihan said. "Tell me, briefly, what you know."

Healey could not refrain from embellishing the tabloids' stories, which he found so richly instructive. Each suspect revealed a serious flaw in Caleb Tuttle's character: the gardener, hired from some work-release program, showed his naiveté, his unwillingness to recognize the fact of recidivism. "Recidivism" was one of Healey's favorite words. He'd loved it since he first heard it at the age of fifteen on "Firing Line," and he still relished the sound of it. The housekeeper's great-nephew hinted at something worse: lust unsanctified by holy matrimony.

"His 'concubine'?" The cardinal interrupted Healey's tale. "The *Times* said she'd worked for him for more than forty years."

"What do you expect from the liberal media?" Most of Tuttle's obituaries had differed greatly in tone from Healey's column and he was chafing to set the record straight. "I believe he brought her over here and kept her no better than a white slave."

"While arranging passage for the rest of her family? How'd the boy get here?"

"Oh, certainly, Tuttle did favors for her relatives." Healey thought the cardinal morally insensitive. "That only deepened her dependence on him. I imagine the boy has extremely traditional ideas."

"Papers say he's a neo-Nazi." The cardinal snorted. "I thought they liked women dependent."

Healey did not address that objection but continued with his story. "I think some members of the family did accept Tuttle's largesse, the housekeeper's niece, the boy's mother, and his father. The American-born boy was prouder, though I'm not condoning what he may have done."

A small fist rapped urgently on a windowpane. Two young faces peered into the room: Julia, the girl who'd come earlier, and a smaller boy. The boy brandished a fishing rod and John nodded, holding up five fingers. The children seemed to recognize the signal and settled down to wait on the porch swing.

"A pretty child," Healey said. "What is she?"

"A little girl."

"I meant her ethnic background." God, Hollihan was provoking, the columnist thought.

"I've no idea. She was a foundling. I baptized her and chose her name. I think it suits her. Five minutes, Mr. Healey."

"I was saying," he resumed, "that, although I have not had, as yet, the opportunity to interview the young man . . ."

"You've tried?"

"Oh, yes, and I expect I will see him soon. My surmise is that he sought to avenge his family's honor."

"I think that is a completely fantastic suggestion. And," the cardinal continued reprovingly, "lacking in charity. Have you any reason to suppose they lived as man and wife?"

Healey shrugged. He hadn't, but he thought he might find people who'd swear to it.

"Well," Hollihan was eager to end this interview. "You may be right about the boy's motive. If he's a skinhead, he's batty enough to believe anything. You came to see me about Father Paul."

"You will not, you *can* not turn him over to the Ukrainians. You must see they intend to sacrifice him, to whitewash themselves, to propitiate . . . potential investors."

"What do you suggest?"

"I'm going to Eastern Europe next week. Let me see what I can find out. Probably," he acknowledged, "some atrocities were committed in the region."

"Jesus, Mary, and Joseph, Healey. I fought in that war. You can take it from me."

Expletives erupted in Healey's head. He'd forgotten that. Hollihan had entered the seminary *after* the war. "If the events were as the Ukrainians represent them to be,

perhaps the true culprit or culprits can be found." He'd
find somebody himself if need be; foreign friends had
already identified people willing to help him find somebody. But that would take time. Healey was desperate
now and driven to speak simply. "Whatever happened,
Paul's innocent. Protect him until I get back."

The cardinal rose from his chair. Standing, he looked
more frail: his thighs were thin above his waders, a flan-
nel shirt hung loosely from his shoulders, and his ring,
which he did not extend for Healey's kiss, seemed about
to slip off over a bony knuckle. "All right," he said, and
went to join the children. He moved deliberately as if
kept in motion by an effort of will.

Healey watched him walk, a child on either side, down
a grassy path to a van the seminarian Timothy Lynch was
loading with children. The cardinal got in the front seat
and rolled down the window. "Report to me, Healey, the
instant you get back."

CHAPTER

7

"No good deed goes unpunished," Nick Hannibal said, coming home after a morning spent studying a sealed juvenile record. "Caleb Tuttle's magnanimity may have been the death of him."

"Do you really think so?" Molly Rafferty was sitting on the living room floor with maps spread out all around her. "Which good deed?" she asked, rising to greet him. There'd been so many.

"To my great shame, fallout from a police discipline case."

"Oh, sweetie," Molly commiserated. She knew this strong man's secret horror: the commissioner thought highly of Nick and broached, from time to time, the thought that he might leave Homicide and apply his good judgment to the thankless squalor and mind-numbing proceduralism of Internal Affairs, the office charged with investigating allegations of police misconduct. "Shall we have wine with lunch?"

"Yes, please. You've decided to go to Krakow?"

"For all kinds of reasons. I've never been there, the topic interests me, and I do want to buck up Wolfi. He

47

called this morning to say that one of the most shameless German revisionist historians has wormed his way onto the bishops' committee. He feels more and more isolated."

Nick told her, convincingly, that he'd miss her but he was glad she was going. You had to stand by your friends.

"I've got to make myself flashcards for the Cyrillic alphabet, otherwise I'll be able to get around in Poland but not in Ukraine," she said, gathering up her maps. "You don't really think Caleb Tuttle was killed by a policeman, do you?"

"I hope not. But Tuttle's gardener," he told her while they ate, "is the twenty-year-old son of a cop called Sparky Sabatini." Sabatini, Molly learned, had been an enduring embarrassment to the department, a pyromaniac if not an arsonist. He went to every fire that came over his radio and many times firefighters had rescued him from burning buildings into which he'd rushed in search of occupants they'd evacuated hours before. He'd caused considerable bad blood between the police and fire departments. When the grievance chairman of a militant firefighters' local had fallen to his death through three blazing floors while Sabatini, unconscious from smoke inhalation, was being taken off the roof by aerial ladders, the mayor stepped in. Sabatini was too young to be pensioned off and he could not be reprimanded for heroism, but he was not to leave the station. He languished in a desk job until a flu epidemic paralyzed the department. They had to put every able-bodied man on the street and his first night out, Sabatini, who never got sick, took on the Boston University hockey team celebrating a victory.

"He's fearless, I take it?" Molly said.

"Was. He's since died, but he was a berserker, an absolute nut. That's where Tuttle comes in. He chaired a blue-ribbon commission that recommended changes making it easier to put men like Sabatini places where they'd do less damage. The patrolmen's union traded the right to pick assignments by seniority for some generous educational incentives. The up-and-coming younger guys liked it because they had the qualifications for the better jobs. Guys like Sabatini felt betrayed. He got careless after that and died in a car crash that violated every conceivable guideline for high-speed chases."

"Have you talked with his son?" Molly sensed that Nick could not long escape Internal Affairs. He assumed responsibility instinctively, and he actually cared about due process. But it would be a wrench, he loved to solve crimes.

"No, I haven't. He's on an island in Penobscot Bay where Caleb Tuttle sent him for six weeks of Outward Bound."

"Beginning when?"

"The next day, you might say. The Saturday after he found Tuttle's body. Tuttle told the Outward Bound counselors when he arranged the trip that the boy seemed restless. There didn't seem to be any reason for him not to go—it was supposed to be a natural death. I've sent somebody to bring him back, just as a material witness at this stage."

They often thought aloud with one another, and Molly was more than usually interested in this case. At the moment, though, erotic impulses distracted her. She wanted to make love before hearing more, so she reached across the table and covered Nick's hand with her own. He stroked and then kissed her palm. They were well matched.

Later he asked her if she'd like to come with him to see Caleb Tuttle's garden, in which Jimmy Sabatini had worked. As they drove there, he told her that Sabatini's court record, especially read in connection with his Department of Youth Services file, pointed in no very good direction. They had to get him away from Outward Bound. Each of the assaults he'd been charged with as a juvenile had been on a person, better educated and better off than himself, who'd tried to help him: a scoutmaster, a parish priest, a hockey coach, two gym teachers, and finally, a female counselor preparing him for a high school equivalency exam. He'd never used any weapon but his fists. Poison did seem a little out of his line, but he might have learned something about it as a gardener.

Anyone Caleb Tuttle taught about plants, Molly thought, walking through the gate that led to his famous roses, might learn a great deal. His garden was remarkable more for its harmony than its splendor, though it was splendid in June, with thickets of iris and peony. There were herbs in abundance: woody thyme and rosemary; the tough perennials, mint, chive, and sorrel; basil, tarragon, and cilantro set out after Memorial Day. Garlic and marigolds repelled insects naturally; grape vines twisted above inviting benches; and, clustered round the pond, grew Tuttle's roses from whose newly sprouted leaves Olia Alexander was plucking beetles to feed to the fish. She asked them to come inside for a cup of tea with her after they finished looking over the garden.

The tool and potting sheds and the garage had been sealed at the same time as the house; Nick wanted to form his own impressions of their interiors before the technicians went to work on them.

"There's enough weaponry here for a major peasant revolt," Molly said, surveying the collection of scythes, pitchforks, and pruning hooks displayed on the walls of the tool shed.

"You're so bloodthirsty," he said. "I see any number of peaceful implements, this little bulb trowel, for example."

"I expect they bring in cow manure for the peonies,"

Molly observed, looking around the shed. "Nothing else is rich enough, but even the commercial fertilizers here are organic: bone meal and some mosses. Nothing toxic."

"Unless it's mislabelled or stored in the wrong container. We're going over the garage tomorrow."

"Why do you think the gardener killed him? Nobody reported any problems between them."

"I know, but all the psychologists who dealt with young Sabatini believe that he hated do-gooders. He told them so. He wasn't one of those tough kids who learn to say what the helping professions want to hear. He believes his father's career was destroyed by high-placed wimps."

"Caleb Tuttle wasn't a wimp."

"I'm not sure a kid like Sabatini would see that."

"And Olia's nephew?"

"I'm doing everything I can to find him. He's been missing since before the murder."

"Nick," Molly said suddenly, "Healey's been here. I thought his column on Tuttle's death was a bit much, even for him—speaking such gratuitous ill of the dead. Now I understand."

"Hmm?" Nick was reassembling a spray gun he'd taken apart.

"Healey wanted people to think he could not write in such terms of a man he'd murdered."

Nick put the spray gun into a plastic bag and stood with Molly, looking from the darkness of the toolshed into the radiant garden. "Are you serious?"

"I'm completely serious. He's been here," she repeated. "Don't you remember that Healey had Tuttle 'sallying forth from his ecologically correct bower'?"

"I'd love to oblige you. He'd make a great villain."

"Nick, he's describing this garden. He had to have been in it, seen it, smelt it."

"Healey's always bashing tree-huggers, babe. It's a subject on which he's occasionally funny."

"That's what I thought, too, at first—another cheap shot he couldn't resist. But look around you. 'Ecologically correct bower' precisely describes it. And there's the kitchen garden—Healey's insufferable 'epicurean *potager.*' Just about every herb that grows in this climate and the most exquisite lettuces."

"I love you," he said. "I've never known anyone to hate with such persistence and ingenuity. Other people are children beside you."

"Talk about wimps."

"Molly," he said. "Let's suppose Healey came here. Interviewed Tuttle. Found him too good to parody, too reasonable. The interview didn't make good copy. He cans it and saves some wisecracks for the inevitable obituary."

"What you suggest is plausible," she said civilly. "Except for the widely recognized fact that Healey's a compulsive name-dropper. If he'd been in an elevator with Caleb Tuttle he'd tell the world. Remember when he was fogged in at Heathrow in the same first-class lounge as George Kennan? He wrote about it for years."

"Okay, how'd he do it?"

"I don't know. You're the detective."

"I think you're right that it would be odd if Healey had been here and kept quiet about it." He was no longer speaking facetiously. "But he's not likely, from what one sees of him, to acknowledge he's been bested in an argument."

"That's right." She was happier to work with him. "If he failed to dazzle Tuttle with his counterrevolutionary brilliance, his readers would never know." Molly readily acknowledged that other motives, discreditable but falling short of murder, might account for Healey's silence. "Still, if you do find out he was here, you'll let me know?"

"I doubt the phones are secure where you're going," he teased her. "Healey must have admirers everywhere."

While she served them tea, Olia Alexander told them that her nephew had not been heard from and raised again her suspicions about the Ukrainian delegation that had met with Tuttle two days before his death. She was glad that Jimmy Sabatini would be coming back from Maine; perhaps he'd seen people entering or leaving the house. He worked fairly steadily, she reported, and though she had not thought him an observant young man, he could not be so completely oblivious as the girl upstairs. She was not a malicious woman and quickly added that the babies were a handful.

Molly was curious about the delegation. Mrs. Alexander had given Nick a list of names, and they were being vetted in Washington. None of them meant anything to Molly.

"Was it a private dinner?" Molly asked. That part of the world was virtually unknown to her, but she'd be there soon. "Were any pictures taken that night?"

Mrs. Alexander said that a photographer from the Center for Participatory Politics had come by and the prints had arrived since Nick first questioned her. She took them from an envelope on a hall table and pointed out to Nick and Molly the man she mistrusted: his fleshy face and glossy pompadour were not prepossessing. Otherwise, the delegation was, with few exceptions, a handsome group, cerebral, soulful, a few restrained *bons vivants* and stylish women.

"Do you think I could get a copy of this?" Molly asked.

Nick shook his head emphatically. One or more of these people could—it remained a clear if unlikely possibility—have killed Tuttle. "No," he said.

This was not the moment, in front of Olia Alexander, to argue the point. Instead, Molly told her she was leaving at the end of the week for Krakow and Mrs. Alexander spoke, informatively, about Galicia. She hoped Molly would come to see her when she returned. She would be glad to hear firsthand about changing conditions.

"Why not?" Molly asked Nick when they were alone in the car.

"You can't carry a group portrait with murder suspects around with you. They may search your luggage."

"I didn't dream of taking it with me. I'll memorize it. I do the freshman class every year, names, faces, and high schools."

"I won't be there."

"That is why *I* need the picture. Nick, you know I'm not stupid or reckless."

No, Molly was neither of those things. She was the quintessential American woman who would venture anything with maps and flash cards. Molly always knew which way was north and where the moon would rise. She drove a standard shift car and carried a Swiss army knife, she was not afraid of snakes, and he did not know what he would do to the man who harmed her.

However, he was not convinced, as she seemed to be, that war criminals or their American apologists had murdered Caleb Tuttle. "There's no good reason you can't have the photograph," he said. "I'm sorry I was such a caveman."

"Your cavemanhood's a good thing, on the whole," she answered. "I do recognize its value."

CHAPTER

8

"Ritter," Hannibal was calling Cologne from his office. "Don't let her out of your sight."

"I will watch her like my own sister. I am sure you know that I love her." Wolfgang Ritter said needlessly sentimental things, and although Nick was relying on his devotion to Molly, he hadn't expected him to be so painfully honest. "I met her some years ago, perhaps she told you. She had another friend then and that friendship gave her much pain, but I was not such a fool as to hope she would turn to me . . ."

So, he's a realist, Nick thought. Molly would not, in any imaginable circumstances, have bolted from that unhappy affair into the arms of Wolfgang Ritter.

"Always we have been soulmates, never has she felt fleshly affections for me, so it will be easy for me, very intimately to watch over her—"

"Ritter," Nick had to cut this short. Ritter's romanticism embarrassed him. "I trust you. I trust Molly. We're all good friends."

"Yes." Ritter shifted to efficiency. "I will meet her plane in Vienna, we will travel together to Krakow, and if she wants to go farther east, into Ukraine, I will be at her service."

"You've done military service, haven't you?"

"Of course. The Federal Republic has conscription."

Good point, Nick thought, as Ritter explained that nonetheless he would not attempt to carry firearms across any European frontier. "I don't expect you to shoot anyone," he said. "Just keep an eye on her and get her on a plane if you foresee any kind of trouble."

"And I will not mention this call."

Nick hadn't felt guilty until Ritter promised silence.

MOLLY WAS busy with last-minute preparations for her trip; she herself was well organized, but several small pieces hadn't fallen into place. A Ukrainian visa, which the embassy had assured her would be no problem, had not arrived. Scattergood College's generally dependable fine arts library had neglected to copy some slides she needed for the talk she was giving in Krakow, and Nick's mother had asked them to dinner and they'd nothing to tell her about their wedding plans.

The slides were promised for four-thirty, not a minute later, and Molly thought she might drive out to the college by way of Hawthorne, the town where Olia Alexander's niece, Iryna Smith, lived with her husband and sons. Mrs. Alexander had mentioned her niece's farm stand; nothing easier than striking up a conversation over vegetables, Molly thought, and so it proved to be.

The Smiths lived in an ample split-level house, with a satellite dish. Several vans, belonging to Thomas J. Smith and Sons, Plumbers, lined the driveway, parked a considerate distance from the basketball hoop above the garage door. Some young teenagers and a large dog were splashing in a good-sized swimming pool. School wasn't out yet, but it was late afternoon, warm and sunny. Plenty of time after dark for homework, if anyone did schoolwork this late in the year. A middle-aged woman sat in the shade, crocheting, behind baskets of appealing produce. Iryna Smith did not strongly resemble her aunt, save in the same look of resolution: compressed lips and steady eyes, set among lines that looked like cracks under the glaze of fine porcelain. Her skin was white and soft, but lined. She appeared to be about forty-five. Molly didn't know how much of her life had been spent in America; she thought Caleb Tuttle had brought Olia's only surviving brother, Karl, to America before 1950. He would be this woman's father, the missing boy, Charlie, named for him. Molly knew nothing about Smith.

She bought some strawberries for Nick's mother and asked about asparagus.

"I'll cut some for you," Iryna Smith said. "Would you like to see the asparagus bed?"

Molly followed her, through tufts of rhubarb leaves, past a hutch teeming with fine brown rabbits, larger, Molly thought, than native hares. A chain-link fence separated the vegetable garden from the swimming pool, and through it Molly saw a well-grown boy jumping up and down on the diving board shouting, "When we're rich, we'll have a bigger pool, so big we can drive a motor boat around it, and water slides in three different shapes . . ."

His mother smiled. "My son has ambitions," she said. "I wish he would remember to feed the rabbits."

About fourteen, Molly thought. She asked his name and was told Thomas. "I know your aunt," she said. "Caleb Tuttle was my teacher, and I've enjoyed your aunt's hospitality."

"You know, then, our worry."

Molly offered tactful encouragement and Iryna Smith continued: "It's ridiculous, about getting rich. We're comfortable here. My husband does very well. People aren't building, or remodelling on any great scale, but with repairs alone, he makes a good living. I keep up the garden and the rabbits because I like to. There's not too much to do at home when your children are teenagers." She separated asparagus fronds, cutting the tender stalks.

"How does Thomas plan to get rich?" Molly judged that an acceptable question, since his mother had mentioned it herself.

"Reclaiming our lost property," she said. "My husband and I both think it's unrealistic. We'd have to be willing to live there, I understand. And I don't think the title's at all clear."

"Your lost property? Here take this." Molly offered a handkerchief to Iryna Smith, who'd cut herself.

"Thank you." She wrapped the cloth tightly around her left index finger and bent again over the asparagus. "Didn't Aunt Olia tell you? Agriculture in Ukraine will be back in private hands, we heard, and at some point in history a large estate belonged to her husband. An agency in Lviv in western Ukraine wrote to us, but we weren't interested in pursuing it."

"Does your older son know about this?"

"He was possessed by the idea." She unwrapped the bandage. "It's stopped bleeding," she said. "I'll rinse out your handkerchief." Iryna Smith washed away every trace of blood with a garden hose, wrang out the cloth, shook it briskly, and returned it to Molly. "We're afraid, my husband and I, that Charlie went to have a look. He has a passport. Before my father died, he promised to take him to Europe if he stayed in school and graduated—and the passport's missing too."

"You need a visa." Molly was acutely aware of this. She hoped an express service was at that moment delivering hers.

"Charlie may not have known that."

"Do you have a picture of him?" Molly asked. "I'm leaving for Eastern Europe tonight."

NICK HANNIBAL found the pesticide he was looking for, stored in an antifreeze can in Caleb Tuttle's garage. The crew that was going over the out-buildings had, until that moment, uncovered nothing more dangerous than ladybugs. Many sets of Jimmy Sabatini's fingerprints and those of the missing nephew, Charlie Smith, furnished by the Hawthorne police, appeared when the can was dusted, and there was no reason they should not. Either or both of those young men might have put antifreeze into Tuttle's Volvo. It was harder to explain why pesticide had been hidden there, though someone who didn't like hand-washing nasturtium leaves might have had reason enough. Nick questioned whether Tuttle had been deliberately poisoned. Perhaps he had inadvertantly eaten some produce that had been sprayed, contrary to his orders, and prepared by someone who did not imagine his orders would be flouted. One would take different precautions, presumably, if toxins were used in the garden and if they were not. Or, possibly, since Sabatini had not been expected to use pesticides, he'd never been taught to use them safely—or reasonably safely, properly diluted, for example.

And why would a murderer leave poison on the premises? It was more likely that an indolent, or skeptical, gardener planned to continue using it.

"Take it back and have the pathologists find out what it can do to you," Nick said, handing the antifreeze tin to a young policeman eager to qualify as a detective. At least, Nick thought, Ignatius Healey hadn't written anything compromising about Tuttle's garage.

Tonight he'd see Molly off with an easy mind. Tomorrow morning he'd find out what sort of rapport existed between young Sabatini and the missing Smith boy. The pattern of the prints did look as though they'd handled the tin at about the same time.

MOLLY AND Nick had dinner with his mother, who forbore from asking whether they'd reserved Queen of Heaven any day in July; she mentioned, however, in passing, that six weeks of prenuptial instruction were currently required before marriages could be solemnized. Nick said he'd always favored on-the-job training, and Molly spent the rest of the meal trying to make peace. Laura Hannibal kissed her good-bye warmly. They didn't see eye-to-eye on everything, but they liked each other.

THE LAST few days had been hectic, and neither Nick nor Molly, facing weeks apart, had much wanted to sleep at night. The wine she drank at dinner made her drowsy, and she fell asleep as soon as the plane was airborne. It took on new passengers at New York, and Molly thought she was dreaming when Ignatius Healey sat down beside her.

"I've seen you somewhere before," he said. "I never forget a beautiful woman."

CHAPTER

9

"Y OU KNOW Vienna?" Healey asked. That city was their
destination.

"Not well." Molly, wide awake now, answered guard-
edly.

"A pity. It's the most enchanting capital. I'd give much
to be your cicerone, your guide." He hesitated an instant,
waiting perhaps for her eager thanks. "Until then, I'll
educate you. I have you," and the look he gave her did
not quite succeed as a leer, "all to myself for eight hours."

He had a point, Molly realized. She could ask for another seat, but short of that they'd be together for the
entire flight. She'd faced this predicament, or variants of
it, in the past—a man, usually it was a man, although
garrulous women were nuisances too, who insisted on
chatting when she wanted to work or sleep. She'd been
inconvenienced before, but never by a person she suspected of murder.

"Ah, *Wien, Wien, nur du alein*." Healey was not musi-
cal. "Vienna, Vienna, you alone, the city of my dreams.
Where shall I begin?"

Not, please, with any more waltzes, Molly thought.

Why not start with Kurt Waldheim and work backward, or begin with the medieval pogroms the city still commemorates, or its beloved mayor, Karl Lueger, from whom Hitler learned so much, or with the Anschluss and the wildly cheering crowds? She'd been in Vienna years before with a lover, a man who later married another woman opportunistically, a lost and no longer lamented sell-out, but, then, irresistible. The city had seemed the most ghastly place she'd ever been in her life. She remembered, most of all, elderly Austrians asking her if she and Danny Bloom were married and giving them, unflinchingly, the answer they clearly expected. She'd be with Wolfgang Ritter this time and she was curious to see how the Viennese behaved if you were escorted by an Aryan.

"One needs to steep oneself in history to appreciate Vienna properly," Healey was saying.

"I'm sure you're right." Molly wondered whether he really did remember seeing her before at the funeral of a celebrated historian, a man in whose death he'd, at best, indecently gloried.

"Are you interested in history?" he asked. If he had seen her at the funeral, he'd seen her in Wolfgang Ritter's company. Ritter wasn't so famous as Caleb Tuttle, but people interested in such things knew he believed in confronting and prosecuting war crimes. Father Paul's defenders must know that too, and it could not be difficult to find out what Wolfi looked like.

"I'm interested in your view of history. You are Ignatius Healey, aren't you?"

"I'm flattered inexpressibly," he said. "I am. My card." The heavy pasteboard bore, as she thought it might, his Gothic logo.

She read the card and returned it to him. She was not likely to need his FAX number. "I thought I recognized you."

"And you?"

She told him her name and he said his mother would approve. "Surely your mother does not concern herself about women who sit beside you on airplanes?"

"She does when I'm smitten."

Touch me, you smarmy little brownshirt, Molly thought, and I'll run you through with my Swiss army knife. "Tell me about Austria."

He talked at great length, exaggerated drivel about Hapsburg statecraft based loosely on misconstrued facts, tacked down by a few accurate dates. C minus. Molly disagreed with virtually all his generalizations, but chose not to contest them. If he asked her point-blank what she did, she'd tell him, but he seemed not to be the sort who asked women what they did.

All through dinner, which he ate and she did not, he praised *Mittel-europa* uncorrupted by liberalism and doubt; when the flight attendant removed his tray, he invited Molly to have a brandy with him. She declined but asked if he could get another cup of rather hotter coffee. He promised to try, and shortly returned with a small pot of excellent coffee.

"The captain's brew," he smiled, pleased with himself. "I autographed one of my cards for the stewardess's parents."

"I do appreciate this."

"You're not like other women." He took her thanks as an invitation to proceed to a more distasteful stage. Why, she wondered, did men think women would be flattered by misogyny? "You are objective, unconcerned about yourself. You seem more eager to learn what I know about Austria than what I think about you."

She truthfully replied that every word he'd said had been a revelation to her. He'd revealed, in fact, most of the prejudices she suspected him of.

"I really do think I've seen you before." He looked at her intently. "In Boston, in a crowd."

The flight had originated in Boston, and she'd been fast asleep when he boarded in New York. It wasn't a very long shot to place her there. Still, Molly judged it time for candor. They hadn't made eye contact when she'd seen him with his notebook at the back of the Arlington Street Church, but he'd obviously been making a careful survey of the crowd. It would be foolish to conceal something he already knew. "You may have seen me at a service for Caleb Tuttle. You wrote a column about him the next day."

"Ah, yes, of course. I remember exactly . . . you were sitting between two men. I envied both of them their proximity to you."

Molly determined to cut flirtation short and move on to politics. "I was with my fiancé," she began, and Healey held up both hands before his breast as if to ward off a blow, "and a friend."

"Cruel, cruel," he exclaimed. "Fate, I mean to say, is cruel. You, my dear, cannot be faulted for failing to wait for me . . ."

Molly managed a self-deprecating smile and continued. "I'm surprised you wrote about Caleb Tuttle as you did, after being there yourself. Weren't you moved by the service?"

"You are afflicted by ecumenism," he said, seizing her wrist as if her pulse would disclose that malady. "Is your dark, handsome fiancé a Jew? I somehow don't imagine it's Wolfgang Ritter you're marrying."

"You know Wolfi?" she said, "He's nice, isn't he? May I pour you another cup?" He relaxed his grip as she reached for the coffee pot.

"I've never actually met him."

Molly told him he might soon have that pleasure: Ritter was meeting the plane. She told him too, as she poured his coffee, stirring in the two packets of artificial sweetener she'd noticed he took, that his question about her fiancé offended her. It was profoundly insulting to suppose women's beliefs depended upon their feelings. She didn't say "people's beliefs" because she imagined Healey thought men more principled. Moreover, she thought, though she did not say this either, that he was wrong. Women were, in her experience, bloody-minded, not light-minded. They were far more likely to seek—or to delude themselves that they'd found—a man who fit their prejudices than they were to abandon them. That, however, wasn't a notion she chose to broach with Healey. "Your question is so outrageous that I wouldn't answer it, ordinarily. I will now, but I expect an honest answer in return."

"Does he read my column?" Healey asked, after Molly told him her fiancé was the Jesuit-educated son of an Italian immigrant and an energetically Catholic mother. She didn't mention that Nick had gone to the University of Chicago after Boston College High. No need to disclose his entire life history.

"Faithfully. And now will you tell me, please, because both of us would like to know, why you spoke so ill of the dead?"

Healey said, a little too pompously Molly thought even for him, that Tuttle had exerted a baleful influence over a prodigious variety of policy areas and that his death did not make his career any less deplorable. "But what was your connection with Tuttle? You're getting married, so you aren't any depraved sort of feminist. You're too pretty for that anyway."

"He was an old teacher of mine."

"Mother of mercy, are you a Kremlinologist too?"

She told him she was not, and that Tuttle had taught

comparative courses about peasant movements. "I know next to nothing about Eastern Europe, or about modern Europe anywhere for that matter. I teach the Renaissance and Reformation at a women's college."

"But that's wonderful," he said. "Much more important than dead Brahmins. You must be going to Ritter's Krakow conference, to which I myself contrived to be invited. I was working on a dissertation on the Counter-Reformation before I was syndicated." He told her about the subject of his work, an Irish monk best known for his defense, in verse, of clerical celibacy, then asked abruptly, "Tuttle himself never married, I believe."

"I believe not. Did you ever meet him?"

"Never. God knows I tried to see him but he wouldn't grant me an audience. I suppose your friend Ritter had an easier entrée. Perhaps you introduced him yourself?"

"No," she said. "Wolfi came to New England to see some Dutch editions of *Pilgrim's Progress*. He's interested in religious narratives." That was at least part of the truth. "He was staying with me and he came to the funeral with us out of respect for Tuttle's reputation."

Talk turned then to the Krakow conference; Healey posed no more questions about Tuttle or Ritter and seemed disinclined to share any but his most predictable thoughts. After a period of patient listening, Molly took out the draft of the paper she was presenting. "This needs another hour or two of work," she explained.

"You're conscientious," he said. "And a reproach to me. I'm only commenting on papers and I haven't read them yet." He opened his briefcase and removed three large envelopes. Two of them, Molly saw, bore clearly printed return addresses, one in Palo Alto, California, the other in Oxford. She knew the Englishman's work, extravagantly mannered and unassailably sound. The third envelope, the only one already opened, had no return address and appeared to have been mailed from Austria.

Healey settled down to read the shortest paper first. He made a few marginal notes, and set it down. That essay from All Souls', Molly knew, would be crisp and combative. You could like it or not, but never fault it on its own terms. The American entry, long and copiously footnoted, looked to have been produced by a conscientious graduate student. The paragraphs appeared to go on for pages. Molly concentrated on her own work while Healey read, grumbled, skimmed, and grumbled again. Midway through the Stanford thesis, he gave vent to a long-suppressed obscenity. Molly looked up.

"Forgive me," he said. "Is there any reason to believe that Mary Tudor was a lesbian?"

"That's a fresh take on Bloody Mary. How are the other papers?"

"Better," he said, taking the third from its envelope. This one was accompanied by reproductions of religious paintings, chiefly, it appeared as he flipped through it, the Marriage at Cana and the Last Supper. People were invariably gathered around a table. "Do you know anything about the symbolic significance of various foods?" he asked.

"Something," Molly said. "This one isn't very subtle." The painting was a sixteenth-century Austrian primitive with Jesus and his disciples, all flaxen haired except Judas, who might have been drawn by Goebbels, about to share a roast pig. "Let's see the marriage feasts. See on this platter. The fig represents lust as well as fertility, because fig leaves in Eden accompany sexual self-consciousness. A pomegranate, alone, might signify simply fruitfulness, but figs . . ."

"I see." Sex, even in a still life, embarrassed him. "This fellow has a theory about shared meals and sociability,"

Healey said. "Most of it's Greek to me. Worse than Greek, unfortunately. I can read Greek. See if you can make sense of it."

Molly read the paper with interest and then turned to a series of transparent overlays, charting egalitarian or hierarchical seating arrangements and identifying in the compositions varying levels of saintliness. The reader was invited to superimpose these over the paintings, but some transparencies did not match any of the paper's illustrations. Molly recalled seeing a photograph of a group sitting around a table that corresponded exactly with one of them. Healey appeared to be dozing, and she was tempted to trace the chart but decided against it. Instead she memorized as much of the notation as she could. She wrote a precis of the paper to justify the amount of time she spent studying it and replaced it in Healey's briefcase.

He woke as the plane began its descent into Vienna. "I regret missing so much as an hour of your company," he said. "Tell me what that happy man, your fiancé, does when you are off at scholarly conferences."

"He keeps busy," she said. "He's investigating Caleb Tuttle's murder."

CHAPTER

10

Jimmy Sabatini wriggled on the hard straight-backed chair, waiting in an ecstasy of self-importance for the lieutenant. To be sitting in the outer office of the Homicide Bureau about to be questioned in a murder case, this was a height he'd never expected to reach. Yesterday he'd been stuck up in Maine eating raw clams and blueberries; worse, he had been told to spread the frigging health food on barnacle-covered rocks to dry it in preparation for a kayak trip with sun-tanned blond youths who hadn't liked their previous education any more than he had. Their old schools, as they described them, hadn't sounded that bad: they got months off winter and spring and most of them had bedrooms right there in the schools where you could bring girls. But they said it wasn't all that great. It was still school. Anyway, none of them had been sprung from Outward Bound to face a murder rap.

He'd tell the lieutenant most of what he knew, and see what he made of it. His dad hadn't made detective, but he knew how they worked: if you told them nothing, they suspected you were holding something back; if you talked too much, they thought you were misleading

69

them. He wondered if Daphne had said anything about
him.

"Hello, Jimmy," the lieutenant said. He was cool. He
came into the station wearing a sports jacket and a shirt
without a tie. If he had a gun, you couldn't see it. He
introduced himself and said he hoped Jimmy would answer a few questions about the days before Tuttle's death.
They went into his private office where he took off his
jacket and rolled up his sleeves. The gun was there, small
and neat, in a shoulder holster.

"You mean murder, don't you?"

"We're reasonably certain Tuttle wasn't poisoned acci-
dentally," Nick Hannibal said. The boy was keyed up,
desperately nonchalant. "But it's a fair question. Do you
think he was murdered?"

"Yeah, I do. I mean he was old. I guess he coulda just
croaked."

"But you don't think so?"

"What I think don't matter." Jimmy seemed at once sly
and crestfallen. He wanted to be pressed a little further.

"You were there the day he died and several days that
week. Anything seem out of the ordinary?"

"I worked in the garden every day that week and I went
inside every day for lunch. When we were alone, Mr.
Tuttle ate at the kitchen table with me, a couple times
he ate in the dining room with a visitor. That was ordinary. But when he died, they took it real hard, old Olia
and Will. I seen them on Saturday when Will drove me
to Maine. Considering how old and sick he was, they
acted like they couldn't believe he was gone. I thought
that was 'out of the ordinary.' "

"That's Mrs. Alexander, the housekeeper, and Will
would be William Flood, the tenant?"

Jimmy nodded. Nick found him more voluble, less hostile than his thick file had led him to expect. But then

cops were one category of grown-up he may not yet have written off. Nick guessed that working lieutenants did not count in the boy's mind as brass. He asked Jimmy about lunchtime visitors. Charlie, old Olia's great-nephew, came early in the week—it must have been Monday, he said, because he'd been late, hungover, after the weekend, and Charlie had gotten there only about half an hour after he had. Two older guys in suits came other days. Not together, on different days. Daphne Robbins, the Reverend Mr. Flood's charmless wife, had also mentioned the nephew had been there that week. Hadn't she also referred to Olia Alexander as "old Olia"? Nick was certain she had, though in a nastier and more slighting way. Jimmy's "old Olia" sounded simply familiar.

"How well do you know Charlie Smith?"

"As well as you can know a nut." They'd argued politics, it seemed. Jimmy thought Charlie was right, maybe, about niggers, but he carried it to extremes. They shouldn't take white guys' jobs, but Jimmy thought sterilizing them wasn't right either. Maybe after too many illegitimate kids, but not just one or two. A lot of guys didn't want to get married right away. "Broads, too."

"Don't want to get married?" Nick had lost Jimmy's train of thought. That hadn't been his experience.

"No, take white guys' jobs."

Don't worry, son, Nick thought. In your lifetime there will be a white male president. How many cops had kids like this? But that wasn't fair. Jimmy, a self-described moderate, rejected Charlie Smith's extremism.

"Jimmy, did you hear Charlie fight with Mr. Tuttle?"

"Sure. I'm surprised you didn't hear him, sitting here in your office in Boston."

"Did he threaten him?"

Jimmy seemed genuinely shocked by the question. "No, Charlie just called him a lot of names and went

storming out. I think Mr. Tuttle wanted to send him to
Outward Bound too," he explained, perhaps in extenua-
tion.

Nick established that Tuttle and young Smith had met
and argued on at least three occasions Jimmy knew about,
but also that Jimmy had not seen him since the Monday
before Tuttle's death. Charlie could have come some time
when he wasn't there; usually he got there himself about
ten and left before five, usually.

"Was that week usual?"

Jimmy said he'd stayed later on Thursday, but had not
seen Caleb Tuttle after about eleven in the morning; he'd
eaten lunch with a visitor. "We thought he went to sleep
early. He did that sometimes."

"Who's we?" Olia Alexander had left the house on
Thursday morning.

"Me and Daphne."

This was said with some bravado and Nick waited for
more.

"You interview her too?" Jimmy asked, and Nick said
he was trying to talk with everyone who'd seen Tuttle
the week he died.

"She's different." Nick recognized this as a request to
hear his opinion of Daphne. "Different" figured in popular speech as an expression of qualified tolerance. The
speaker hadn't encountered anything like it before and
wasn't favorably inclined, but would, for the moment,
keep an open mind. He asked Jimmy how Daphne was
different.

"She's friendly, like," the boy said, leaning back in his
chair, expansive, worldly, "real friendly."

Nick asked a personal question, crudely.

"Sure I did. Jesus, she wanted it. Her husband was never
around. But it ain't my kid. I didn't get there until April."
He went on to say that she made him use condoms because of something she called STDs and he didn't like

them but they were better than no sex at all. "She said it was okay to have sex because she was pregnant. The baby was Will's, so, like it wasn't taking nothing away from him."

Nick recalled the University of Chicago's excellent introduction to Western Civilization: some canny old pagan, Hume he thought it was, made a good case for feminine chastity after menopause even though indiscretion could not, in that season of life, produce wrongful heirs. He wondered what Daphne read at Bennington. "When did you leave on Thursday night?"

"About eleven. I was pretty bombed, but I don't think anybody else was in the house."

Nick had nothing more, for the moment, to say or to ask about Daphne Robbins. He thought that if Tuttle knew about the affair he'd most likely do just what he'd done: get the boy out of town. He might have spoken an avuncular word to Flood about spending more time at home. He might even have reproached Daphne, more mildly than Nick would have liked to himself, about loosening the boy's already shaky grasp of conventional morality. Nothing Nick knew about Tuttle suggested he'd threaten either party with exposure. His next question dealt with pesticides. "Charlie Smith's parents grow a lot of vegetables."

Jimmy said maybe they did. They lived in the country, but he never went out to their place.

"Charlie ever help you with Tuttle's garden?"

He said he hadn't.

"You like cars?"

Jimmy, predictably, yearned for a red Camaro. "I seen a bitchin' black Camaro, used," he said. "The guy who owned it had to sell it to make bond. But I couldn't afford it. I'm kind of glad. I'm gonna look around and get a red one."

"Work on Tuttle's car?"

He said, no, it was a foreign car and Tuttle always took it to the same mechanic.

"Your fingerprints and Charlie's are all over a can of antifreeze we found in Tuttle's garage."

"What the fuck would we be doing with antifreeze?" Jimmy asked. "I didn't start working there until April."

Nick told him that was a good question.

"So, what about Miranda? Don't you have to get me a lawyer?"

"We can stop now, and you can get yourself a lawyer. You can't get a free, court-appointed lawyer unless I charge you with something, and I won't do that because you're not guilty of anything except lying."

Jimmy was disappointed but vastly impressed. "You know about the organic shit?"

"All about it, the slugs so nourishing for the fish, the edible flowers. Your spray gun's at the lab."

Charlie had brought a big can of pesticide from his parents' garden in Hawthorne, Jimmy admitted. The Smiths used it and then waited awhile before selling from the plot they sprayed. Jimmy hadn't dared keep the whole can anywhere on Tuttle's property, so he and Charlie decanted it into several containers: the antifreeze can had been found, the wine bottles in the cellar had not.

Okay, Nick thought, that was easy. Now, who else knew about the new pesticide in old bottles? "Was anybody else in on this?"

"Hell no, you think I'm crazy too?"

"Daphne?"

"Yeah, sure, we had a couple of laughs over it. But she wouldn't tell nobody."

"Did Tuttle usually have salad at lunchtime?" Nothing lethal had turned up in the bottles of vinegar or oil, but Nick was still waiting for an analysis of the teak salad bowl; its unvarnished surface absorbed oil and if pesticide had been mixed, for example, into a strongly flavored vinaigrette, traces would remain in the wood.

"Almost always—they ate rabbit food all the time." Jimmy remembered a wooden bowl. He didn't think Olia and Tuttle ever used a different one at lunchtime. He didn't like salad and never ate it.

"Just a few more things—did you leave before the big party on Wednesday?" He said he had, although he'd stayed to help the college-kid waiters bring up some cases of wine from the cellar. He'd left before any of the guests arrived. No one then, except Olia Alexander, was available to testify about the Ukrainian delegation. The waiters were, unfortunately, an idealistic group of Marvell College roommates who'd left for Central America before the crime was suspected. Nick had their names but no reliable way to reach them. "What do you remember about the other two noontime visitors?"

Not much, it appeared. The first guy, Jimmy figured, must have come on Tuesday, because he wasn't there on the same day as the noisy fight with Charlie Smith or on Wednesday, the day old Olia was cooking for the big dinner. Nick knew that was right. He'd spoken with the Tuesday guest, a foreign service officer who'd shown Tuttle still photographs of the Zborodny massacre and several posed and unposed picture of Father Paul, the earliest taken in 1949. Tuttle had been unable to reach any conclusions and made arrangements to see the films as soon as possible. A screening had been planned for the following week, the Monday or Tuesday after his death. Tuttle had apparently said, and this strengthened Nick's respect for his shrewdness, that it was easier to alter features than gestures. A man's gait or his habitual postures rarely changed. It was also possible to tell, without sound, what language a man was speaking from the way he used his hands and shoulders.

The second man? Jimmy drew a blank. It was Thursday, so Olia had already left. Nobody had seen Charlie since about two o'clock on Monday afternoon and old Olia beat it out to Hawthorne the morning after the big dinner. He'd had lunch up at Daphne's; she'd given him some money and he'd gone to get Tex-Mex take-out. She didn't like to cook and she liked hot stuff. He'd told her you are what you eat and she said in that case he'd better clean his plate. After lunch, she turned on the TV for the kids and they went to bed for maybe an hour. Nick thought a liaison more depressing than theirs would be hard to imagine. "But you're sure Tuttle had a guest for lunch or around lunchtime?"

Jimmy said a taxi had let somebody off about noon.

"Man or woman?"

"Man, definitely." With suit, tie, and briefcase, Jimmy added. He'd seen him from the garden, where he was weeding the lettuce, looking forward to hot stuff.

"Tall or short?"

"Short."

"Light or dark?"

Jimmy couldn't remember.

"Caucasian?"

"Oh, yeah, sure he was white."

"Do you remember anything about him at all?" Nick asked. "Don't try to imagine anything. Just give it a minute and try to think back."

"As he was coming up the front walk, he stopped and looked at the flag pole, like he was surprised to see Tuttle had an American flag."

Okay, babe, Nick thought. One for you. "He was short. Was he small? Thin? Wiry? Did he look like a shortstop?"

"Hell no. Pudgy, lardball." Jimmy, muscular and well proportioned, spoke contemptuously.

Nick arranged to visit the Tuttle house with Jimmy in

the morning to locate the wine bottles containing the rest of the pesticide; they hadn't turned up the first time the cellar was searched.

He'd been asked to spend the afternoon at headquarters with the captains planning for a projected disaster, the level-funding of the Homicide Division in the new fiscal year. The budget session took all afternoon and most of the evening, so he didn't see the morning paper until late that night. He was leafing through the *Globe* waiting for the Red Sox to play in Oakland when he saw Healey's column, datelined *En route to Krakow*. For the first time in his adult life he felt something like panic.

CHAPTER

11

IN THE MORNING, Nick realized he'd overreacted. Ignatius Healey may have met with Tuttle the day before he died. He was inclined to credit Molly's intuition about that, but he wasn't ready to leap with her from lunch to murder. He didn't know for certain when Tuttle ate or drank what killed him. Even assuming Healey were involved—as principal, accomplice, or possibly as a horrified witness unwilling, as he seemed in another case, to trust in due process—Molly wouldn't be in any danger discussing the Reformation with him. Not unless he also killed people who held different views on the priesthood of every believer. The woman he loved was protected by an American passport, a stalwart friend, and her own highly practical intelligence. He ought to get a grip on himself and go to work.

But he ought to check it out. The flag story was evocative and Jimmy Sabatini couldn't have made it up: who but a man like Healey would be surprised to find Tuttle a patriot? He made two calls before he left home, one to put some heat on the slackers with the salad bowl, another to start checking cab companies.

Jimmy Sabatini had been told to stay in town available for questioning and he'd seemed pleased to matter that much and eager to help. He was waiting, freshly shaved and wearing a clean tee-shirt, at Caleb Tuttle's cellar door at nine o'clock sharp.

The cellar had been gone over thoroughly, fairly thoroughly, once before. It was clean and dry, if not obsessively tidy, and the search had found nothing suspicious: odd pieces of furniture, chests and steamer trunks, crates full of ice skates, a horsehair sofa, a dining room table too big and too heavy to give to poorer relations living in modern houses, and a small amount of fresh litter—junkfood bags, candy bar wrappers, cigarette and reefer butts, some empty bottles of a cheap, domestic light beer and vodka nips. The trash suggested that Charlie Smith might have stormed noisily from Tuttle's house and crept quietly back. He might have spent a night or two on the horsehair sofa, waiting to approach the Ukrainians about his fancied legacy. Would any of them have trusted him with the smallest task once apprised of his lunatic views? "Did Charlie Smith drink these brands?" Nick asked Jimmy.

"Everybody drinks 'em," Jimmy said, and Nick knew what heavy-metal kids smoked.

The wine cellar occupied about a quarter of the basement space and extended beyond the foundations of the house. Its racks were arranged by continent, country, and region; Nick wasn't surprised his crew hadn't found the pesticide the first time they looked. They had spot-checked the bottles and found none of the good vintages tampered with. The boys hadn't, Jimmy explained, attempted to remove and replace the foil and cork on any of the fancy stuff; instead they'd poured out home-brewed fruit brandies, labelled and dated in Olia Alexander's spidery hand, and substituted Bug-Off. There was no perceptible difference in color, and Jimmy wasn't sure exactly how many bottles they'd used, not more than five or six: after opening dozens of bottles and sniffing—the plum brandy smelled good, the pear very good—they located three bottles full of pesticide and another about three-quarters full. Pieces of broken bottles had been swept up and dumped into a trash barrel: heavy green and brown glass, but also some clear fragments with the handwritten label still attached. Three cc's of pesticide taken straight would kill you quickly, Nick had learned; mixed with oil, which would retard digestion, more would be needed and the process would take longer. It was impossible to tell with any certainty how much was missing.

A portion of the cellar wall, brick rather than the original stone, marked the entrance to the tunnel dug in the 1840s to bring fugitive slaves back and forth from the riverbank. That much information about the Tuttle House appeared in all the guidebooks. Several of the bricks were loose; Nick had checked them his first day in the house and established to his satisfaction that a child could not have passed through any of the open spaces. He'd then called a local antiquarian society whose director, a woman with a cultivated voice, told him a bit more. The river entrance to the tunnel silted up every few years. It had been a technical challenge to keep it open in the decades before the Civil War, and the Tuttle family had appealed to a Yorkshire mine engineer, a member of the British Anti-Slavery Society travelling in America, to prop it up. Under his direction, the tunnel had been timbered like a mine shaft. During Prohibition—the woman's voice took on an edge at this point—the timbers were removed and the cellar entrance bricked over. Caleb Tuttle's father wanted to make certain the haven was not abused by a local rum runner whose business and political ethics he deplored.

Nick said he hoped the police had been grateful for his

cooperation; the woman chuckled and said she'd be happy to cooperate with him.

"Jimmy," Nick asked. "Did Charlie ever brag to you about getting rich?" He'd been mulling over Molly's account of her visit to the Smiths' vegetable stand; the boy's mother said he'd been "possessed" by the idea of some foreign legacy. Who'd fired his imagination?

Jimmy was dumbfounded. He'd been impressed when Nick figured out he'd been spraying the vegetables, but this time Dr. Watson himself could not have been more agreeably abject. "Jesus," he gasped. "You know everything. You bug everybody's phones with satellites, right? Charlie said you could. With no wires or nothing?"

"The technology's pretty good," Nick said. "But most of it's illegal . . . even for the police."

"Yeah, tell me about it." Jimmy knew from his dad that search warrants were for pussies. "How do you really do it? I mean how many guys does it take to listen to all the crap people talk on the phone?"

Nick explained, patiently, that wiretaps were used in a limited number of circumstances, usually with the owner's consent. He was sure Jimmy didn't believe him. "You see yourself," he said. "It wouldn't work to have half the people eavesdropping on the other half. Nobody'd get any work done."

"But you know about Charlie's . . ." He'd been skeptical himself when Charlie told him he was getting a castle. "About all the land and stuff?"

"I know a little. Not as much as you do."

"Charlie said he could get rich if he could get back to the old country."

"He talk to anybody from over there?"

"He was sorta secretive about the details . . . I think maybe he did. But that wouldn't make him kill Tuttle, would it?"

Nick had no answer for that question, but he was

curious about Charlie's contacts with visiting Ukrainians.

"He ain't gonna be a movie star too?" Charlie had boasted of so many things.

"Not that I've heard." Nick had trouble taking any of Charlie's ambitions seriously, but the junk-food wrappers suggested that he might have stuck around, at least until Wednesday. Once Nick had established that the tunnel couldn't be used to leave the house, he'd dismissed it from his mind. Now, he thought he ought to see if anything had been hidden behind the loose bricks. The preservationists had been emphatic that nothing archeological in nature could take place in the Tuttle House without them. Maybe it was time to call the knowledgeable woman and ask her to stand by while they tore down the wall. In the meantime, he'd drive out to Hawthorne where Olia Alexander was staying with her niece.

THE TWO women were sitting, a bushel basket on the grass between them, in the shade of a fine old tree. They were shelling peas, calming themselves with a simple, shared, repetitive task. They looked up as Nick got out of his car and walked towards them, and both continued to reach down into the basket, bending and rising, carrying on their work as they turned their attention from it.

Nick reported that he had no news of Charlie, only some ideas he'd like to talk over with them. Iryna Smith thanked him for all he'd done to help them, and he said he wished he'd had better success. He wanted to be honest with them, not alarm them or exploit their trust. He wasn't sure how to proceed and sat down on the grass at their feet. He'd been mulling this over on the drive and reached no conclusion.

"Have some, Lieutenant." Olia Alexander passed him

a handful of pebbly green peas. "They're good raw." She was a gracious woman, hospitable as Demeter, difficult to imagine as the battered bride of a lout. She represented an entirely different aspect of rural life, and Nick was reluctant to shatter the peace she'd created for herself. He ate the peas gratefully, like a child at his mother's knee.

Iryna Smith had some of her aunt's strength, or resignation. "You have no real news, but, maybe, an inkling of bad . . ." She wasn't frantic, but alert and apprehensive.

"Nothing solid, and nothing really worrying," he assured her. "But I hope I can ask you about his arguments with Caleb Tuttle. You don't have to tell me anything."

"I think we should do whatever we need to do to find him." Olia Alexander wasn't giving advice, simply speaking her mind. "I believe he's in more danger if we don't find him."

"My husband and I have discussed it," Iryna Smith said. "We hope it's coincidence, his disappearing just before Caleb died, but there's another coincidence that frightens me."

Nick anticipated something like this. "Somebody else stopped looking for Charlie shortly after he stopped coming home?"

"Yes." His mother's answer was exhaled, as if she had been holding her breath. "A man stopped calling for him. At first, I was afraid he wasn't calling because he knew Charlie was dead."

"Iryna," Olia spoke in gentle reproof. "No need to expect tragedy."

"I don't. I'm always frightened the first twenty-four hours he's missing, each time he's away. Then I remember he doesn't like to tell us where he's going. He's eighteen. He could enlist in the army or get married. He doesn't need our permission to stay out all night."

Olia urged her niece to tell the detective about the calls that no longer came.

"The caller asked for Karl," she said. "And I told him my father was dead. After that he asked for 'young Karl.' He never called him anything else. He didn't sound like an old man, or old enough to be Papa's contemporary."

"American?"

She wasn't sure. She'd never had an extended conversation with the caller. She was certain it was the same person each time. He said nothing while waiting for Charlie to come to the phone and he hung up whenever he was told Charlie wasn't there. She wasn't sure when he began calling her son; she thought she had first taken a call from him about two months ago. He seldom phoned more than once a week and had not called since the morning of the day Charlie left, the Monday before Tuttle died.

"How did you first learn about the Ukrainian property?"

"One of our neighbors saw an article in *Time*, about people reclaiming their family's house in Czechoslovakia," Iryna said. "She showed it to me and asked me whether I thought anything might belong to us. I said no, my grandparents were poor."

"My brother and I," Olia added, "never imagined ourselves as heirs to anything the Germans promised my husband."

"But you eventually got some sort of official notice, didn't you?"

"No, a group in Lviv wrote to us asking for money. They claimed to be researching deeds on behalf of claimants in our position. When we checked with the embassy, they'd never heard of them."

"Iryna and her husband thought it was a scam," Olia said. "I thought it might be worse than that."

"Political?" Nick suggested. He'd grown used to assuming that characterful women never forgot or forgave historic wrongs.

"Of course." Olia split several peapods and stripped them cleanly. Her busy hand recalled Madame Defarge. "Think, Lieutenant, what kind of Ukrainian would solicit money from families whose claims dated from the Occupation?"

"I'd like to trace the calls Charlie got," Nick said. "I'd need your consent."

"Please," his mother said. "Whatever he's done, I want to find him."

CHAPTER

$$\boxed{12}$$

MOLLY RAFFERTY was walking with Wolfgang Ritter on the Gänsehäufel, an island in the old Danube where people came to row and swim. On a Sunday morning in June, picnickers, sitting and lying on blankets, crowded its grassy banks: Viennese burgher families, some American and German tourists tired of museums, waiting for the pastry shops to open, and mingled with these comfortable shapes, the leaner, darker bodies of Turkish and Slav guestworkers. "Vienna's more attractive than I remember," Molly said. "More polyglot." It was her second day in the city, but she'd slept through most of her first, after the excitement of an overnight flight with Ignatius Healey.

"I agree," Ritter said, "but most local people do not. They call the city 'balkanized,' if"—he spoke very low— "if they are too polite to say 'mongrelized.' Not many are that polite."

"Nobody here believes in hybrid vigor, I guess." Molly loved the beautiful, incongruous faces of American children. "Didn't you think Healey was excessively cordial?" She turned from tender thoughts to her more pressing worry.

Ritter had met her plane at the gate on some pretext he'd not yet explained. She was travelling with just a carry-on bag and she'd hoped to lose Ignatius Healey in passport control or customs. Instead, she could not avoid introducing him to Ritter and he'd immediately invited them both to join him for dinner, not that evening—he suffered terribly from jet lag—but tomorrow, Sunday.

"We'll rent a rowboat, shall we, Molly?" Ritter asked. "If we row far out into the stream, we can speak freely about him." Ritter, who'd been horrified to see Healey follow Molly off the plane, was taking every precaution. Like Nick, he judged it hardly possible the columnist had killed Caleb Tuttle to prevent him from identifying Father Paul, but he thought it would be better—Vienna was in his opinion a very bad place—that Molly not be overheard making that case.

"I'd love to row."

They made their way toward a dock piled with dull ochre-colored boats. "Maria Theresa yellow," Ritter said. "It's a jaundice one sees everywhere."

A sign informed them the concession was closed for lunch. The woman who rented boats would be back at 13:30; they sat on a nearby bench to await her return, talking about the Reformation, because, Molly gathered, Wolfi would not let her talk about more recent controversies until he'd gotten her out of earshot of the shore.

They chatted until a newly arrived couple caught their attention, a couple who seemed vastly content with their common task, first spreading a commodious blanket, covering most of it with an embroidered cloth, and then unpacking the largest picnic hamper Molly had ever seen. The husband and wife worked together in wordless harmony, arranging several varieties of sausage, two loaves of dark bread, a dozen kaiser rolls, three jars of pickled cucumber and onions, some hard cheeses, a pot of butter and a pot of mustard and a crock of cold sauerkraut. Four two-litre bottles of beer and two glazed pottery steins decorated with scenes from the Austrian Alps appeared after the food was in place.

"Where's the rest of the family?" Molly whispered as the woman cut a thick wedge of liverwurst and spread it on a thicker slice of bread. "They can't eat all that themselves." The wife, slightly less corpulent than her husband, handed him the first appetizer and made another for herself.

"The children have probably grown up and left home, if they had any at all. You'll see, they'll eat most of it."

The pair ate methodically; the man drinking noisily from two successive bottles of beer, ignoring the stein which his wife encouraged him to use. After each sip she took from her stein, she touched her lips with a linen napkin.

"I'd say no children," Wolfi said after watching them gloomily. "The Viennese birth rate is low. That's one of the reasons they hate foreigners so much; they're afraid they'll outbreed them."

As if in fulfillment of that vision, a boy and girl speaking some soft slurred tongue—"Serbian, I think," Wolfi said, catching the sound but not the meaning of their words—came down the path hand in hand. They carried neither blanket nor basket, and flung themselves onto the grass, rolling over each other almost to the water's edge, passionately kissing. Molly wished them whatever joy they could find in Vienna: their play was more demonstrative than she'd wish to be in public, but by no means obscene. The youth appeared to bite the girl's neck; she flung back a head of magnificent hair and arched her back voluptuously. Then she rose to her feet in one graceful motion, pulling her lover up beside her. She seemed to be reminding him they were not alone; they embraced, standing, for some moments and ran off to a grove of trees.

The good frau was not amused. "Slavs," she said loudly. *"Kein Delikatesse."*

No delicacy, Molly thought. She sets a high standard herself.

"Slavs," the woman repeated, appealing to Molly who sat, pale, fair, and cool in green linen on a bench, not even touching her blond friend. *"Schwein,* they are pigs, are they not, *fräulein?"*

"I'm sorry. I don't speak German," Molly said, rising. Wolfi took her arm and led her to the rowboats, whose proprietress had fortunately returned. She sensed that if he could not have rented a boat at that moment he would have stolen one.

"That's what I remember about Vienna," Molly said, after Wolfi had rowed them speedily away from the landing stage. "How unapologetic its racism is. May I have an oar now?"

He made room for her beside him. "The Austrian couple shocked you."

"Americans have prejudices, but, with the exception of Ignatius Healey, we don't voice them so openly. I prefer our way, even if it is hypocritical. Civility remains the norm."

"That contempt for Slavs cost Germany the war. If they . . . we . . . I suppose I should say Germans of that generation . . ."

"Wolfi, you can say 'they.' "

"If they could have been even civil to the conquered peoples, like the Ukrainians who hated the Russians, they could have stabilized the eastern front, set up little Vichyite puppet states in many places."

"Then, I suppose we should be grateful they couldn't."

"So." Wolfi bowed in the direction of the river bank. "I thank them. Now, tell me about Healey. We will row nicely together and keep our backs to the shore so our lips cannot be read."

"You musn't tease me too. Nick's been merciless. He says I'd frame Healey to discredit him."

Molly and Ritter spent most of the afternoon on the river talking about Caleb Tuttle's death. Molly knew that much of what she said was far-fetched, but Wolfi listened indulgently. He was interested to learn that Healey'd asked whether he himself had met with Tuttle; he was also very interested to hear that Healey was carrying transparent diagrams that might be superimposed over group portraits. He added some suspicions of his own about the housekeeper's great-nephew.

"If the boy has neo-Nazi leanings would we belong to an organized group? I was wondering if membership lists would be available, perhaps for the wrong sort of Ukrainian nationalist looking for American sympathizers."

"Perhaps not just sympathizers"—Molly recognized that her thought was more than far-fetched—"possibly recruits, for some dirty deed."

"The parents had a letter, you said, from Lviv about some property. Maybe the boy was promised more, a title or something."

Molly had not thought of a title as an inducement to the sort of boy she imagined Charlie to be; she considered it now, resting her oar and dipping her hand in the water, which was not blue but pale grey.

"Duke Charlie? Count Charlie?" Ritter shrugged his shoulder. "Why not? Would it strike such a boy as foppish?"

"I'm not sure how it would strike him. In any case, he probably doesn't realize republics don't have dukes."

"Why should Ukraine remain a republic? These people may have other plans."

This was an obvious point, Molly realized, coming from a European. Americans take so much for granted. We don't begin to imagine the full range of possible debacles.

"Wolfi," she said, sure of his sympathy if not his approval. "We've time to go to Lviv, haven't we, before the conference?"

"Molly," he said plaintively. "Molly, yes, there is time."

"Please."

"Let me check the timetables. And we will say nothing to Healey tonight. I'm not sure you should have told him as much as you did." They were still sitting side by side, each with an oar. He glanced, fondly, at her and saw her cheek was pink. "You've had enough sun," he said. "Let's turn back."

They heard sirens when they were still far down the river, and, as they neared the dock, shouting and screaming. Riot police were pulling youths, some in brown shirts, some in white shirts with swastika armbands, away from the people they'd attacked, foreigners with complexions darker than their own. Ritter kept the boat in mid-stream until order had been completely restored.

"I've never actually seen a riot like this," he said, ashen-faced. "I've seen a thousand newsreels and television clips. It's hard to believe it's happening when you actually see it."

"Nazi organization and insignia are tolerated in Austria, aren't they?" she asked. She was stunned by the apparent ferocity of the attack. She knew that facial wounds bled heavily, so possibly people were not all so badly hurt as they seemed; but several of the guestworkers looked to be seriously injured. These men, she saw, were asked to produce documents which the police minutely examined before permitting ambulance crews to treat them. She noted, too, that few of the attackers were detained and not because they ran or skulked away. Most of the skinheads strolled off, laughing, arm in arm.

CHAPTER

$$\boxed{13}$$

"I HOPE YOU had a pleasant day?" Healey had reserved a table at a restaurant which may not have been the most ostentatious in the city. Its walls were covered with flocked crimson velvet and its tables set deep into red plush booths. Silk tassels and gilt ropes hung everywhere, and no piece of glass that could be cut or faceted had escaped, save for silvery mirrors set in heavy ormolu frames above each booth. The management promoted the belief that an upstairs room had been a favorite trysting place of the lamented Crown Prince Rudolph.

"We were at the Gänsehäufel," Ritter told him.

"There was a disturbance there, I heard. Nothing distressing for a lady, I hope?" Healey was all solicitude. "Fortunately, you were not alone."

"We were on the river," Molly explained. "The police had everything in hand when we got back. They were checking the papers of the injured while the Hitler Youth slipped away."

"One can hardly blame them. It's very trying for a settled community to absorb so many immigrants with such different and often most provoking customs. Americans can sympathize with that, as," he turned from Molly to Ritter, beaming, "as do also our friends in the Federal Republic."

"But you yourself would not deport all immigrants." Molly was not asking a question. She was reminding this xenophobe that he'd not toss suspected war criminals out the golden door.

"No." He smiled and opened the menu. "They know me here, why don't you let me order?" After fussily instructing the waiter, Healey returned to his theme: "I understand that case-by-case review may be impracticable. In the case of deepest concern to me, that of Father Paul, I have done my modest best to serve the ends of justice."

"You have moved earth and heaven," Ritter said.

"And you have tried to," Healey replied. "Ritter, I know that you're in touch with Cardinal Hollihan. He did not tell me that in my most unsatisfactory interview with him, but I know from other sources the lies you've fed him."

Ritter rose. "Would you repeat what you have just said. I thought I heard you say I lied."

"I didn't say that." Healey, unperturbed, took up the wine list. "What duelling society did you belong to, Ritter? Sit down."

Ritter remained standing and Molly gathered up her bag and jacket, ready to leave with him.

"Oh, sit down," Healey said. "I didn't say you lied. I said you fed the cardinal lies. You passed along to His Eminence information I know to be untrue. I don't insist you knowingly lied."

"Do you apologize?"

"Of course. Goodness, you people are touchy."

"Historians must defend their reputation for truth-telling," Molly said.

"That's what I meant, my dear. Ritter's a most distin-guished German historian and I've asked one of his col-leagues, my good friend Schluessel, to meet us here to help me reason with him."

"I will not drink with Schluessel," Ritter said. Helmut Schluessel was a military historian whose most recent book urged that civilian casualties during the Second World War be understood in the "context" of total war. He played fast and loose with census data and life-expec-tancy figures to show that fewer Poles had died between 1939 and 1944 than in any other five-year period since 1800. Jewish mortality, he acknowledged, had been a tri-fle higher, but he suggested there might be other explana-tions for these data: higher suicide rates and a greater incidence of anxiety and depression were hypotheses he explicitly advanced. Sexual aberrations, he hinted, sapped vitality.

"As you wish," Healey said. "But I think you'll want to hear what he has to say."

"I've read his book. I know what he has to say." Molly was now determined to leave.

"I'm only concerned that you both hear what he knows about Father Paul. Schleussel is positive that he cannot be the man the Ukrainians are looking for."

"I would not believe anything Schluessel said about the eastern front," Ritter said. "If he said summer followed spring I would doubt it."

"I will listen to what he has to say," Molly said. "But I will not meet him socially."

Healey guessed rightly that Molly would insist on this and resigned himself to having a very late dinner that night. He asked the waiter to clear the table. "I'll have the cloth removed too if you like, my dear."

"I would prefer it."

Helmut Schluessel arrived, somewhat chagrined to find a green baize surface where he'd expected something more festive. He'd been looking forward to several dishes the menu advertised as favorites of Crown Prince Rudolph. Nonetheless, when Healey told him a business meeting would precede the meal, he opened his briefcase and produced a sheaf of documents purporting to show that Paul Szlepensky had been born to Polish, not Ukrainian parents.

All parties agreed that the frenzied killer at Zborodny had been a Ukrainian, not from Zborodny itself but recruited from a smaller village for a special unit in which Poles were not permitted to serve, and Father Paul was, beyond dispute, a Pole. Here was the marriage certificate of his parents, the civil record of his birth the next year and of the births of siblings in subsequent years, the parish register in which his baptism and first communion were recorded, enrollments in school and in confraternities of pious youth, even some yellowed photographs. Schluessel set these out chronologically, offering a careful account of the provenance of each piece of evidence.

Schluessel was a tall, thin, grey-haired, grey-eyed man; his exposition went on, unhurriedly, as if he did not expect to be interrupted with ill-considered questions. He has to be completely bloodless or very bloody indeed, Molly judged, to think and write and speak as he does.

"And if the documents do not convince you," Healey said, after Schluessel had laid them out like Tarot cards on the table, "think about your responsibility to Holy Mother Church. No Catholic priest or layman can afford to call into question the agonizing political choices the Holy Father made in that terrible time. We are contesting now, with the Orthodox Church, for the souls of the former captive nations."

"Examine your own conscience, Ritter." Molly felt the chill in Schluessel's voice. This was not a kindly exhortation.

"You must abandon this vendetta," Healey said.

"You are unjust," Molly protested. She knew, or thought she knew, what Healey and Schluessel were getting at. Wolfgang Ritter's grandfather had, as a member of the Catholic Center Party, voted in the Reichstag for the Enabling Act. The Center had voted *en bloc* to give Hitler extraordinary, extraconstitutional powers; that measure, duly voted, was all the new chancellor had needed to consolidate his power. A few months after the passage of the Enabling Act, the papal nuncio signed a concordat with Hitler, insuring, among other desiderata, state subsidy of Church schools, a concession the Vatican had been unable to wrest from any Weimar cabinet.

Ritter's grandfather, who had followed party discipline in this matter, came to believe his vote had been a tragic mistake. His remorse led him, his children believed, to take a walk along the Rhine during an air raid ten years later. His body had never been found.

"You cannot wash out your family's shame with the blood of this innocent preist," Schluessel said, ignoring Molly.

"Or whiten your past by blackening the Church," Healey added.

"I believe that what is dirty can be made clean," Ritter said. "But not by more lies."

"How much of the truth do you want told, Ritter?" Healey's cherubic face had become a gargoyle visage, taunting, malevolent, "My friend Helmut tells me the truth is sometimes fatal in your family."

The four were seated on a circular bench in a booth, Healey and Molly next to each other in the middle, Ritter and Schluessel in the outer places. Ritter got up and asked a waiter who had been hovering since Schluessel's arrival, hoping to take his order, to get Molly a cab.

"Wait for me in the cab," he told her. "If I am more than five minutes, go to your hotel. I'll call you when I'm finished here."

"I'd like to stay." She pressed his hand.

"Go, please."

She went but only as far as the door.

"So." Ritter turned to Healey. "The truth is fatal."

Schluessel smiled, a more ghastly smile than Healey's. "Suicide has been, regrettably, almost as common in your family as among the most degenerate groups."

Ritter lunged across the table at Schluessel and seized him, not by the throat but by his narrow shoulders. Grasping him firmly, he threw him against the gilt-framed mirror hung above the plush banquette. The mirror shattered, and Schluessel fell back down onto the seat.

Ritter saw that he was conscious and repeated to him an expression familiar to them both: "*Keinen Schuss Pulver wert*, you are not worth the powder and shot I would need to kill you."

CHAPTER

14

No one attempted to prevent Ritter from leaving the restaurant. He expressed his regret to the proprietor that an accident had caused the mirror above his table to break and pressed upon that astonished man a round sum in Deutschmarks. Molly, who had seen the accident from the foyer, was waiting for him.

"The cab's here," she said.

He got into the car with her and said a word to the driver, who seemed pleased with his instructions.

"Where are we going, Wolfi?" Molly asked as the car shot off into the Favoritenstrasse. She thought she'd begin with an easy question.

"To an even more quaint and charming restaurant. It's outside the city, so the driver expects a good tip."

"Will we have the rest of the evening to ourselves?" They were hurtling around the Ring and turning north toward the villages in the Weinerwald that offered tourists evenings of wine-tasting. She'd seen that assault was not always prosecuted in Vienna, and perhaps expensive restaurants preferred not to involve the police in their patrons' squabbles.

"The city is ours to enjoy," Ritter said. He was sure Schluessel would be too embarrassed to press charges, but he wanted to make himself conspicuous that evening. "I'm taking you to a delightful place in Kahlenberg."

"Whatever you think best." She'd never suspected a violent streak in Wolfi. No one was more gently or bemusedly ironic. No one more saddened or less surprised by cruelty. She knew he'd debated Schluessel before, in public. He'd reviewed his books. Their arguments had been, hitherto, bitter but correct; the decorum they'd both preserved struck her as surreal, considering that their quarrel concerned the murder of millions of people. What could Schluessel have said to him tonight?

"I will explain myself, Molly, when we get there," he said, as the cab left the brightly lit streets and entered the partly suburban, partly bucolic outskirts of Vienna. "It will be easier in a crowded, public spot."

Molly pondered this. Wolfi had something to tell her that he preferred not to say in private: did he not trust his composure if they were alone? Or was he protecting her from some awkwardness that might follow his confession?

The cab pulled up in front of a rustic inn and a valet in Tyrolean costume hastened to open the car door. "*Gruss Gott*," he greeted them, Viennese-fashion, and led them to the first of a succession of genial hosts who took them eventually into a garden hung with colored lanterns.

"The service here," Ritter said, after they were seated at a table surrounded by wine-making apparatus, geraniums in wine barrels, waitresses in dirndls, and gypsy violinists, "is grovelling and inefficient. Germans like it because it reinforces their traditional views of Austria, and the Austrians take some comfort in not being Prussian."

A group of German tourists at a neighboring table began to sing a limited repertoire, lustily.

Molly looked around the garden. Who would tell the gypsies to play the *Marseillaise*?

"There's no piano player either," Wolfi said, reading her thoughts. "But Schluessel will not be able to say he could not find me."

Molly waited for her friend to begin. He drank some of the thin, cold, greenish wine the restaurant featured and broke a roll into small pieces. The waitress had not yet brought butter.

"My father killed himself."

"How old were you?"

"Seven. He hanged himself. I was in the country with my grandmother and I stayed with her afterward because my mother found it difficult to be alone with a child."

Molly spoke a few words of comfort, words whose inadequacy she painfully felt. Seven. A boy of seven. God. Molly had long known about grandfather Ritter, the anguished failed democrat, but she had not known this: that Wolfi had lost his father and also, in consequence, a mother who'd gone mad or abandoned him when he was a little boy. Nick's father had died tragically too, when Nick was young, but Laura Hannibal was a strong and brave woman. "And you know why your father . . . ?" Wolfi was about forty; he'd have been seven well after the end of the war.

"Yes."

There was a lull in the singing, and a trio of violinists stopped at their table to inquire whether, like all couples, they had a favorite tune. When neither of them replied, the musicians fell back on "The Blue Danube." The pair was so unresponsive, they switched to *"Che serà, serà"* midway through the waltz. Molly tipped them, and they went away puzzled. Guests were rarely so hard to please.

"My father was a regular army officer, although the distinction between army and SS was much less im-

portant than people like Schluessel pretend. The army
was up to its eyes in slaughter. But it isn't true either that
it was death to resist. One could always request transfer
into combat; and officers sent home any number of men
who couldn't bring themselves to kill civilians, usually
on some medical pretext. Most of them probably thought
the sensitive souls were bad for morale. Others may have
sympathized. In any event, my father sent home more
than his share."

"So was he disgraced? Recalled?" The patriotic songs
had resumed, and Molly moved her chair closer to Ritter's. His story should not be shouted above this din.

"No, he was a clever tactician and his superiors protected him. After the war, when his military ability was
of no value, talk began. People said he'd sent home fragile
beautiful boys, his homosexual lovers. My grandmother
told me that the men he'd helped did constantly come to
see him, that they idolized him.

"As one would expect."

"As one would also expect, rumors fed on their visits.
My grandmother told me this much later, naturally, and
she gave me the letters he wrote to my mother from
Russia. They read as if he wrote them to a woman he
loved. Do you think I was wrong to read them?"

"No." Molly shook her head. "No, I don't. Children
have to have parents. If their letters were all you had, you
needed them."

The waitress brought sausages and dumplings and Ritter sent her back for the grilled trout they'd ordered. She
returned minutes later saying she'd forgotten whether
they wanted cabbage and spaetzele or potatoes with the
fish. As she made her way back to the kitchen, a new-
comer joined the party at the next table, interrupting their
song. He appeared to make an announcement. A murmur
of approval ran around the table and one of the men who'd

been most joyfully carolling came over and shook Ritter's hand. "Good for you," he said. "Schluessel may be right about the war but he had no call to say that to you." He bowed to Molly and withdrew, saying he'd intrude on them no longer.

The trout arrived, encased in some rococco pastry crust, and Molly said it would be fine. "News travels fast, Wolfi."

"What do you make of Schluessel's dossier?" he asked her, boning his fish deliberately.

"It's got to be fraudulent. It's too complete."

"You're right. It's next to impossible to recover prewar marriage and birth records. The German army systematically destroyed local archives to obliterate all memory of an independent Polish state. Virtually every public building in Poland was burned." The singing had begun again and they bent almost cheek to cheek to continue their conversation.

"But the forgeries are good, aren't they?" Molly spoke low. She thought one of the German women had been watching them.

"Extremely good. It's the sheer number that calls them all into question."

"I half expected he'd produce affidavits from people who'd spent the day of the massacre in prayer and fasting with the accused." The woman had gotten up from the table and gone in the direction of the ladies' room.

"Paul's supporters are saving those for the trial," he said. "Prayer, but not fasting, of course," he added and she thought he was joking.

"They might convince some people with the documents," Molly objected. "But nobody'd believe a witness who swore Paul was somewhere else during the massacre. What would make a day fifty years ago memorable?"

"Don't you know when it happened?"

"In August of '42."

"August fifteenth."

"The Feast of the Assumption," Molly said. "You were serious; it's not a fast day."

"They'll produce eyewitnesses," Wolfi predicted. "Wait and see. Do you think you'll want dessert?" Another, more buxom waitress stood by with a pastry tray.

Molly thought she would not and asked him to excuse her for a moment; the woman was, indeed, powdering her nose, with unpressed powder from a heavily jewelled gold case. "Ritter's views are *weibisch*," she said, meaning weak and womanish. "But he is not. I am sentimental. I hope you will together find happiness." She snapped her case shut and left before Molly could reply.

Wolfi rose and seated Molly when she returned. "One of the women choristers," she said, "is also a well-wisher."

"I'm glad for her support," he said, adding up the bill and finding errors in his favor. "Would you give me Nick's phone number, Molly, before we leave? I want to ask his advice about something."

Molly suggested they call together when they got back to the hotel, and Ritter resisted—he wanted to call Nick himself and apologize for the situation he'd put Molly in. But before the manager had the bill sorted out, she'd persuaded him that the three of them should talk things over.

"VIENNA ALL you remembered it to be?" Nick was in his office, mulling over some new developments that made Molly's suspicions about Tuttle's death more plausible than they'd initially seemed. A cab driver, who listened to a lot of talk shows, distinctly remembered picking up Ignatius Healey at Logan Airport late in May and dropping him at a big house in liberal la-la land. They'd had a helluva talk on the ride in from the airport; Healey was a helluva guy. He oughta run for president.

"All I remembered and more," she said. "It's been a full day today. And I sat next to a celebrity on the plane. Ignatius Healey."

"Where are you calling from?" So, Healey was not only en route to Krakow, but actually in Vienna.

"My hotel room."

"Is your colleague with you?"

"Yes."

"I'm in the middle of something," he said. "Why don't you call me from the train station tomorrow morning?"

He knew she'd planned to fly from Vienna to Krakow. "Fine. We'll talk later." She turned to Wolfi. "He wants me to call from a public phone."

"Let's go out for pastry. That will be even more public than the other places we've been."

CHAPTER

15

Nᴄᴋ Hᴀɴɴɪʙᴀʟ sat with his head in his hands waiting for the phone to ring. He'd made arrangements to check the line as soon as Molly called back. Now there was nothing to do but wait. He wasn't a rash or impulsive man, but he feared that if he moved from his chair he might start throwing objects against the walls of his office. Inaction, which he hated, was better than action he'd regret.

The case against Healey was by no means watertight. He'd seen Tuttle within twelve hours of his death and he'd concealed that fact for weeks, although it was common knowledge that the police were appealing for information about Tuttle's last days. He'd been with Tuttle around lunchtime; lettuce prepared for salad had been eaten, and a barium-based pesticide that would cause irregular heart beats dangerous to an elderly man with Tuttle's cardiac history had leached into the teak salad bowl from which that lettuce had almost certainly been served.

But it was the phone call to Charlie Smith that convinced Nick Ignatius Healey had to be looked at seriously. Healey was not, it turned out, the caller who'd regularly asked for "Karl." Those calls had been traced to a motel in McLean, Virginia. The desk clerk said a man came every couple weeks all spring; he paid cash and made no trouble. No dames, no trace of dope of any description, not even any bottles. He signed in as "Mr. Barbarossa, F. Barbarossa." The clerk thought it might not be his real name because he didn't look Italian, but who cared where you came from if you paid your bill and left the room clean.

God bless America, Nick thought. He got a description of F. Barbarossa and relayed it to the people at the State Department who were looking into the background and recent whereabouts of the Ukrainians who'd met with Tuttle. Some hours later a desk officer called excitedly to say he'd discovered "Barbarossa" had been the code name for the German invasion of Russia in 1941. Nick, who'd passed along the information solely for that reason, hoped there were others working on the case.

Healey was not Barbarossa—he'd been tall and gaunt—but possibly they knew each other. When Healey himself called Charlie Smith, he'd done nothing to conceal his identity. Nick had found this out by a curious fluke earlier that day.

Iryna Smith, who, he believed, was cooperating with him unreservedly, had found a telephone number, written in her younger son's handwriting on the back of a copy of *Sports Illustrated* under his bed. When she questioned Tommy about it, he'd forgotten jotting down the number. When she pressed him, he remembered. A man had asked for Charlie, but he'd called after Charlie'd been missing for a while and Tommy'd said he didn't know when to expect him.

Mrs. Smith had called Nick with the number, a 212 area code—she didn't think Charlie knew anyone in New York. The operator had said 212 was Manhattan—and

Nick had hurried out to Hawthorne to see Tommy, who, after his mother left the room, spoke frankly about his older brother.

"He's a fuck-up. The man told me Charlie should call him collect any hour of the day or night. Like it mattered. Like anything Charlie did could matter. I said 'sure' and forgot it. Mom thinks he'll come home. I don't care if I never see him again."

"What about your dad?"

"He gets kinda tense when Mom's unhappy. He says Charlie'll outgrow it." Tommy seemed to doubt that the passage of time would do much for his brother. Iryna Smith just wanted to find him alive. Her hopes for Charlie's future, Nick gathered, centered on this minimal wish.

Nick thought the call should be returned, most suitably by Charlie's parents, who, if the caller seemed at all reasonable, could appeal for news of the boy's whereabouts. He would like to listen, however.

"Should we wait for my husband to come home?" Iryna asked. "Don't you think this person might take men more seriously than women?"

"Possibly, but if we're dealing in stereotypes, worried mothers ought to rate some consideration."

She smiled ruefully. "I can do without that kind of consideration. I'll call from the kitchen. There's an extension in Tommy's room."

Tommy's room was plastered with pictures of NBA stars. "My brother's an asshole," Tommy said. "Can you believe he thinks whites are better than blacks? I mean *physically* superior?" He sat down on the bed. "Can I stay?"

"Sure." Nick picked up the phone and listened as the 212 number rang.

"This is Ignatius Healey's office. Would you like to

leave a message? Mr. Healey's abroad but he checks in
for calls every evening."

"I'm not sure I should trouble you," Iryna said. "Mr.
Healey called my son, who hasn't been able to get back
to him."

Nick covered the speaker with his hand. "Tell your
mother Healey should call her. Hurry." The boy thudded
downstairs to deliver his message, and Iryna asked, firmly
but not urgently, that Mr. Healey call her at his earliest
convenience.

All this had happened since Molly left two days ago. It
was five o'clock in Boston now, midnight in Vienna. She
must have understood she should call him back right
away, but not from any place she was known to be staying. What was keeping her? Ritter was with her and he
was tougher than he looked. Nick checked his watch. It
had been only ten minutes since Molly'd hung up.

Nick got up and walked around his office. He left the
door open so he could hear the phone when it rang and
went down the hall to get a cup of coffee. The coffee in
the pot smelled stale and scorched; somebody had taken
all but the last inch and forgotten to switch off the hot
plate. He decided against making a fresh pot; he didn't
want to miss the phone while he went farther down the
hall to get water.

Back in his office, he picked up Tommy Smith's *Sports
Illustrated*. It was the June fifth edition, which New England subscribers would have gotten in the mail around
June 7 or 8. Tuttle had died on May 27; so this call could
not have come before he'd been dead for more than a
week. By that time, it was public knowledge that he'd
not died naturally. But Healey might also have been in
touch with Charlie before that, perhaps through an inter-
mediary. Nick took out a calendar and tried to fit Healey's
call into a sequence with Barbarossa's. No pattern
emerged.

Fifteen minutes. How far did you have to go to find a phone booth in Vienna? The pencil he'd been writing with snapped in his hand.

"HANNIBAL," he said, grabbing the phone.

"Nick, I'm having such a good time, but I miss you terribly." Molly was calling from an ornate phone cabinet, screened from a candlelit pastry shop by white velvet curtains. Wolfi sat at a table from which he could keep an eye on the phones and the front door.

"I got messages that you called."

"Just to hear your voice, darling," she said, "and to tell you how much I wish you were here."

Nick's answer, a parody of melancholy love, warned her to proceed cautiously and they exchanged affectionate inanities until a buzz of static interrupted them.

"The line's okay, babe," he said. "I was having it checked. Let me catch you up."

When he finished she told him her suspicions about Healey, that he'd claimed Tuttle refused to meet with him and pumped her about contacts between Tuttle and Ritter. She did not know what to make of the transparent diagrams Healey carried with him; possibly they were the key to some new evidence he hoped to get. "And speaking of evidence," she said, "we were presented with rather a lot of it tonight, Wolfi thinks none genuine, purporting to clear Father Paul."

"By Healey and this colleague of Wolfi's?"

"Yes, the infamous Helmut Schluessel. Wolfi wants to tell you about Schluessel himself, but he had appalling provocation, and he's taking precious care of me. It's interesting you suspect people in Lviv are involved with Charlie Smith. We thought we'd go there tomorrow."

"Let me talk to Ritter." Wolfi had provocation? What did he do, raise his voice? Nick was surprised he'd done

even that in Molly's presence, and he was astounded
when he heard Ritter's story. "This side-trip to Lviv,"
Hannibal asked, after they'd talked about the broken mirror. "Do you know anyone there? Anyone you trust?"

"A woman I trust completely. I know Molly will like
her. She's an Enlightenment scholar and a great enthusi-
ast of Joseph II."

"Refresh my memory on Joseph II."

"A reformer. The only anticlerical Hapsburg."

"Molly will love her," Nick predicted.

"More to the point. She was one of the Ukrainians who
dined with Tuttle. She's an adviser to the committee
that's drafting the new constitution."

"That could be helpful."

"I sincerely hope so," Ritter said. "But, Nick, I am of
two minds about something else and I thought you could
help me think it through. Also, I believe you have rights
in the matter."

"I hope I can help," Nick said, mystified. He can't be
thinking of declaring his feelings, in some decently dis-
embodied way, before Molly's actually married to me?

"Should I arm myself?"

"Can you?" Nick was relieved to hear a professional
question. "I thought you told me you couldn't carry arms
across a border?"

"I'm not sure I can." Wolfi had looked into this. "But
I can get a permit to hunt in Poland. Hunting's a big
moneymaker for the Poles. Germans pay large premiums
to shoot game, elk principally, in the national forests.
It's so many thousand Deutschmarks per point for their
antlers."

"So you could get a gun legally once you were there?"

"That's right. Whether it would be wise is another
question . . ."

"Isn't there a season?" Nick couldn't imagine that the

most cash-poor country would permit hunting in early summer before young animals were weaned.

"For deer and elk. Wolves can be shot all year round, but foreigners can't collect the bounty." Ritter's research on this as on other subjects had been painstaking.

"So, you must decide . . ." It was a tough call. "What would you do if Molly weren't with you?" Nick asked.

"I'm not sure. Probably go unarmed. I don't think a gun offers much protection. But it offers some."

"If Tuttle's murderer, or murderers, want to kill again, I can't see it being a shoot-out," Nick said. "Besides, an attack on you, the German most associated with the attempt to try Father Paul, would be stupid. Virtually an admission that his backers have something to fear."

"These people are not all so clever. You know the joke about the three kinds of Nazis?"

Nick had not heard the maxim, which went like this: There are three kinds of Nazis—honest, intelligent, and loyal. But no single Nazi can be all three.

"It may not be wholly fair to apply this to Healey and Schluessel," Ritter said. "But I believe they are both intelligent. About this Charlie Smith and some of the Ukrainians, I'm not so sure."

"Get a gun."

"Thank you, my friend. I don't have to tell you . . ."

"No," Nick said. "You don't."

CHAPTER

16

ᴇ**ARLY NEXT** morning, Wolfgang Ritter paid a substantial fee to Polish consular officials in Vienna and received a hunting license valid for one year. "I beg the gentleman, might the gentleman sign the ledger," the clerk asked in Polish.

Ritter recognized the polite oblique form of address; that usage, "I beg the gentleman," with the word "gentleman" in the accusative case, was highly formal but easy to remember. Calling a person by his first name, on the other hand, required the speaker to learn the maddeningly variable vocative case, *Pawel* became *Pawlu; Piotr, Piotrze;* and *Barbara, Barbaro.* He'd memorized six cases of dozens of common Polish names.

Ritter and the clerk, who courteously supplied correct grammatical forms whenever Wolfi faltered, were both pleased to complete this transaction without lapsing into German. "The other gentleman"—the young diplomat felt that man fell short of Ritter in more than one way— "spoke no Polish at all."

Ritter signed the ledger just below Helmut Schluessel's name. He decided he and Molly would not go directly to

Lviv. They would rent a car and drive to Budapest and continue by train.

"THIS HIGHWAY'S so American," Molly said. "It's virtually a strip."

"The better way to go from Vienna to Budapest," Ritter told her, "is to take the hydrofoil down the Danube. But that takes longer. We'll be in Budapest in a couple of hours."

They'd crossed the frontier, a perfunctory stop at a decidedly post–Cold War checkpoint, and changed money and drank espresso on the Hungarian side at the neon-lit NON-STOP RESTAURANT, open 24 hours, English and German spoken. The dual highway on which they were driving, built in anticipation of a 1996 Budapest World's Fair, was lined with shops, motels, and gas stations. Kiddie-rides, gypsy caravans, and souvenir stands adjoined many of the service stations and most of the motels. From time to time, women in peasant dress stepped perilously close to oncoming cars, flagging down their occupants with cut-rate fox skins and fringed shawls.

The city of Budapest was very much more restrained and elegant; while waiting for the evening train to Lviv, Molly and Wolfi crossed and recrossed the Danube on the city's beautiful bridges and took the subway to the National Gallery, where they saw a premier collection of Spanish painting, some curious biblical scenes by Jan and Pieter Brueghel, and the original of the Last Supper with Roast Pig that Molly had first seen in the possession of Ignatius Healey.

TRAINS FOR the east left from Keleti Station, built in 1884, when Budapest was, with Vienna, twin capital of the Austro-Hungarian Monarchy. Keleti, artificially lit with cheap dim bulbs, looked like the maw of hell. In its cavernous spaces, shifting throngs of people clustered in small groups, broke apart, gathered again. Runners darted through the crowds; an occasional gangly American with earring and backpack, clinging to his Eurail Pass, asked for the train to Venice or Salzburg.

Molly had never seen so many vicious-looking people in one place: Smugglers, pickpockets, prostitutes, blackmarketeers, money changers speculating in the rising and falling rates of newly decontrolled currencies. It was this, Molly concluded, the impression that travel was prompted exclusively by greed or vice that gave the station such a hellish aspect, at once squalid and sinister. She'd stepped from an urbane city into an underworld without pretenses. Here was crime seizing opportunities so raw, so immense and unprecedented that its pioneers had not troubled to tack on a facade of respectability. Clearly they needed none; policemen did not even enter the station, though some patrolled the taxi stands.

"Moscou, track one." Molly read the board. "Is that ours?"

"Yes, the train goes all the way, making many stops," Wolfi said. "That's why we see so many smugglers. Traders, I should say." He was nonjudgmental about other people's customs. "There's no reason why people shouldn't sell what little they have. That's what the West has been preaching to these poor people for decades."

"You're very fair."

"The ticket agent said it's a green train. This must be it." It was a long train, many cars, most still stencilled CCCP but otherwise fully international: WAGON-LITS, SCHLAFFEN-WAGON, CARROZZA-LETTO, the sleeping cars displayed most of the languages of the Common Market. "I reserved a first-class compartment," he ex-

plained as they passed many cars, none first- and few even
second-class, looking for car number two, seats numbered
7, 8, 9, and 10.

Molly had noticed that she was holding four tickets.
These were all she was carrying, because Wolfi believed
the baggage to be his responsibility even though she
prided herself on packing lightly and never travelled with
more than she could carry comfortably herself in a bag
with a shoulder strap. He followed therefore, a few paces
behind, burdened somewhat with his luggage and hers.

"I took four tickets, so we'll be alone even if they've
put in the upper bunks."

"Upper bunks in first class?"

"I hear they only put four in first class when the train
originates in Moscow, but I thought our privacy was
worth the extra tickets."

It was a very long train and the first-class sleeping cars
were at the farthest end, close behind the engine. A guard
checked their tickets carefully before permitting them to
board and the tickets were examined again by a train
matron, grim and officious, before they were allowed to
pass from the corridor of the train into their compartment. Once in their compartment, she demanded, in
what soon emerged as a pan-slav lingua franca, "*documenta*," passports and visas.

When the matron withdrew, Molly wasn't sure what
they had done to displease her. She didn't think people
who checked tickets and passports expected to be tipped.
Perhaps she thought people of different nationalities and
different surnames should not share sleeping compartments? Wolfi, not surprisingly, drew another conclusion.
"She's younger than fifty, wouldn't you say? But her parents must have suffered terribly and told her of their
sufferings."

This is going to be a nightmare for him, she thought.

His own guilt-ridden *Drang nach Osten.* "Wolfi, maybe the railroad's getting more efficient and laying people off. Maybe she's worried about redundancy."

"Molly, you are so sweet."

They left their compartment door open, watching other passengers board. Molly was struck by the dinginess, not so much of the car, which was, she thought, about as clean as Amtrak, but of the other first-class passengers. Two women, surely mother and daughter, struggled down the corridor with one suitcase, several shopping bags, and seven or eight enormous bundles, which seemed to be collapsable baby carriages wrapped in bedspreads or thin blankets and tied with heavy cord. Others carried even more irregular packets, the contents of which could not even be guessed at.

Passengers had paid about one hundred and fifty dollars in some convertible currency for their tickets, more doubtless if they were going all the way to Moscow; this was an enormous sum. Wolfi had said his friend in Lviv, a tenured professor at the University, earned the equivalent of about fifteen dollars a month. So, these smugglers or traders were not working with a low overhead. Would they supplement their dealings with political intrigue? A great many things must be for sale in Eastern Europe now, she thought. She asked Wolfi idly if he didn't think it would be easier to smuggle in second class. The train crew wouldn't have time to scrutinize each passenger so carefully.

"There will be time to search every passenger and every compartment," he said. "The train will stop for several hours at Čop."

Molly unfolded a map of the former Soviet Union and found Čop, pronounced "Chop," at the base of the Carpathian Mountains, on the frontier between Hungary and Ukraine. "Will the border formalities take that long?"

"The railway gauge changes," he explained. "The

tracks are farther apart in the old Soviet territory. We'll be hours at the frontier while they switch the undercarriages of each car to put on wider axles."

The frontier, he showed her on the map, had been east of the Carpathians before the war, but once the Russians had gotten their tanks, with much blood and toil, through the mountain passes and headed across the plains of Hungary and Czechoslovakia toward Berlin, they stayed. They understood the terrain; they'd have been fools to do anything else.

"And the railroads were never standardized?" Molly asked. "Even within the Warsaw Pact countries?"

"It may have been too expensive a project," Wolfi said. "Or maybe they tolerated the inconvenience to make sure the Motherland itself stayed hard to invade."

THE TRAIN began to move, close to on time, and Molly heard a promising clatter in the corridor. The woman who'd taken their tickets came in with steaming glasses of tea set in shiny tin holders, which in Tsarist days had perhaps been silver in first class.

The tea was too hot to drink and Molly studied its tin holder. "Look how eclectic it is, Wolfi." Vine leaves and bunches of grapes were embossed on its handle and on the rings that encircled the glass; a medallion suspended between the rings presented a more complicated though still conventional image of scientific progress: a rocket rose trailing an arc of exhaust toward a crescent moon; the globe beneath, small and round like an orb, was surmounted by a building that hedged its bets with slightly bulbous towers, suggestive both of onion domes and factory chimneys. A sputnik orbited over the horizon, just above the building's main excrescence and beneath the rocket's tail.

"Soviet iconography will be studied now," he said.

"Now that its god has failed. This is an interesting artifact." He examined his own glass of tea and then looked
searchingly out the window. Night had fallen before the
train left the station. "Later," he said, "we should turn
out the lights and try to see something of the countryside."

Molly could see little beyond their reflections in the
glass. But the plains did look very flat; tanks going in
either direction could proceed at a good clip.

The matron collected their tea-glasses and showed
Molly a white enamel boiler at the end of the corridor
from which some passengers were filling mugs for instant
coffee. The prospect of washing with hot water was a
pleasant one, and shortly later the matron brought towels
and bed linen, coarse and worn, with faded peasant motifs
printed rather than embroidered along its borders.

"Shall I make up the beds?" Molly asked. Their seats
faced each other, a table between them, a twin-bedded
arrangement; hooks were suspended above the seats to
accommodate another bunk above each berth, but these
were not in use on this trip. A folding ladder, wedged
between the seat and the wall, reached to an overhead
shelf where mattresses, blankets, and pillows were
stowed.

"You should get some sleep, Molly," Wolfi said, taking
down one mattress only. "I will sit up."

"The compartment locks from the inside," Molly observed. "There's no need for you to stay awake."

"Let me watch over you," he said. "Indulge me in this."

She asked him to wake her at Čop, but that turned
out to be unnecessary. The train made several stops, and
Molly woke briefly each time, until the chugging rhythm
began again. At Čop, the train stopped and the cars
lurched forward and back, with tremendous clashing and
jolting. Molly sat up. Wolfi had turned off the reading

light the better to watch the activity outside. The platform and sidings were brightly lit; and heavy winches, used perhaps only for freight cars, stood idle beside the track. The sleeping cars were jacked up, one by one, while workers hammered, clanging and sparking, loosening the western undercarriages and sliding the eastern width, with more shudders and jolts, into place.

All the hammering was not taking place on the platform: along the corridor, Hungarian border police were rousing sleepers—surprisingly, some of those roused claimed they'd been sleeping—rechecking documents and searching compartments. They climbed onto the shelves where the bedding was kept and lifted each seat, exposing unsuspected hiding places beneath. They did not, however, ask Molly to open her bag; nor were they concerned with Ritter's. Molly saw, as she stepped into the corridor, that the guards were more thorough with the packages belonging to the now very rumpled and frowsy mother and daughter, the baby-carriage brokers who'd gotten on the train at Budapest. They eventually unwrapped and rewrapped all eight bundles; as they finished with each, the daughter crossed herself three times.

There followed a lull. After an hour of strenuous labor on the platform and calm aboard the train, another group of Hungarian functionaries came through, checking currency declarations. After they departed, the mother and daughter both crossed themselves.

The train had been idling at Čop since midnight; Ukrainian customs officials, raffishly handsome young men, arrived at about three. The first contingent dispensed quickly with Molly and Wolfi's papers, though one of them did return to count the stones in Molly's ring, a thin circle of reddish Florentine gold set with old rose diamonds. She'd never thought to count them herself; but she verified the number and agreed as the guard scribbled "12 d." on the bottom of her currency declaration. The next set of guards paid less attention to their baggage.

The mother and daughter in the next compartment experienced difficulties with both groups; after another thirty minutes or so, when all activity outside the train had ceased and only signalmen remained to wave the engine on, an older, weightier, evidently senior Ukrainian officer appeared, in a better-cut overcoat with broader lapels and three stars on each shoulder. He stood talking with the two women in the corridor—there was a problem with the documents. *"Problema"* and *"documenta"* must be universally understood, Molly thought. She was interested in the man's demeanor; he looked at the mother's passport and spoke at length, without bluster, calm rather than implacable, accustomed to exercising authority and not dissociating himself from it. He did not seem to be saying "Madame, if it were up to me . . ." Rather he was elucidating the problem and seeing no solution.

Finally, he fell silent and the daughter reluctantly agreed. *"Pravda,"* she said. "True." The mother and daughter conferred, calmly and at length, still in the corridor, and finally the older woman took up the one actual suitcase among their bundles and followed the officer off the train. On the platform, they joined the four or five passengers who had presented or encountered a problem in second class, among them, Molly was virtually certain, the missing youth Charlie Smith.

He was standing, a thin boy in a stained and rumpled white shirt, a little apart from the others under a lamp that emphasized his scruffiness. Charlie had been clean-shaven in the picture his mother had shown her, but now a mustache that might have been a smudge darkened his upper lip. He set down the black gym bag he'd been carrying and looked around the platform, as if he expected to meet someone. Minutes later, as the other passengers filed into the blockhouse that served as police station and customs shed, a woman strode onto the platform and escorted him to a waiting car.

MOLLY AND Wolfi speculated about the possible meanings of this rendezvous until dawn, when daylight forced them to admire the strangely familiar beauty of the Carpathian foothills. Like Vermont without public libraries, Molly thought; the train followed a rocky streambed, full of rushing water on both sides of the track. Deciduous trees showed bright early leaves, but only the highest hills remained wholly forested. Pastures had been cleared far up the steep hillsides; dark, giant shapes lurked in their grey mist. As the light grew stronger, haystacks emerged made of new cut grass, shining green and gold and piled impossibly high. "How can they stack the hay so high?" Molly asked.

"It must be drying on some sort of rack," Wolfi suggested. "You see how misty it is; the fields must get very wet at night." Shortly later, as they passed a cluster of cottages, they saw the solution. In the village, where grass was less plentiful, parts of the hay-frame remained visible. New-mown grass was hung over a teepeelike arrangement of spiked poles, leaning against a smooth central stake.

It was six o'clock; they were due in Lviv at eleven. "You sleep now, Wolfi," Molly said. "It's bright daylight, we've passed the frontier, and I've got to learn the Cyrillic alphabet."

CHAPTER

17

"Lviv was always *weltbürgerlich*, cosmopolitan," Marta Tsevchenska had greeted them exuberantly as they stepped from the train, embracing them both, Wolfi whom she knew, Molly whom she'd just met, and sweeping them off to a tiny car driven by a man she introduced as Bogdan, a paleoanthropologist. "This afternoon we shall take you on a tour and you will see."

They were going to the Intourist Hotel where she'd booked rooms for them. Another, better hotel, she apologized, was full of entrepreneurs and people pretending, more and less convincingly, to be entrepreneurs. Marta Tsevchenska's vivid presence filled the cramped interior of the little Volga sedan; she was handsome and spirited and she looked almost exactly like her picture. She was the tall woman with the sleek chignon and slightly prominent light eyes who sat on Caleb Tuttle's right at dinner.

Bogdan had been sitting farther from the head of the table, but Molly recognized him too: Bogdan Soltan, who Marta said found Bronze Age tools in the environs of the city, pushing human habitation back much farther than previously claimed, had a fleshy face with a mole between his round black eyes and another mole on his chin and glistening black hair combed into a pompadour. He beamed his assent as Marta Tsevchenska continued in praise of their city's pluralist past. Beyond question, he was the man who'd roused Olia Alexander's suspicions.

"Lemberg, as it was called under the Hapsburgs," Marta said, ignoring the more recent period of Nazi occupation, during which German was spoken in the city, "was the capital of Galicia. Poles, Germans, Tatars, Jews, Greeks, Armenians, Turks, all lived here together amicably, or for longish periods fairly amicably—we don't claim to be better than other people. Lviv was an important link in the trade routes between the Black Sea and the Baltic. We've always been *weltbürgerlich*."

Though she spoke the witty, qualified English of a first-rate scholar, Marta Tsevchenska again chose the German word "world citizen" for this generous notion. Marta had put Molly in the front seat with Bogdan; she sat in back, pressed close to Wolfi by the luggage, and she seemed to be talking chiefly to him. Very promising, Molly thought; her warmth and energy would be wonderful for Wolfi. Chiefly, however, she was thinking about Bogdan, who seemed about to speak.

Very haltingly, clutching the steering wheel in two enormous hairy hands, he turned to Molly. "The city sites itself on a riffer."

Molly had wondered about that. The guidebook placed Lviv in the valley of the river Poltva, a tributary of the Bug; she'd found neither stream on the map and no sign of water between the train station and the hotel before which Bogdan had just stopped the car. "Where is the river?"

"Under the ground," he said. "In pipes."

"A whole river in pipes?" Ritter asked.

"A big pipe," he explained, wrenching the parking

brake into its locked position. "All the old houses are connecting with it. It is the city's gut." He leaned across to open Molly's door and then got out himself and began unloading the luggage. Ritter attempted to help him but he insisted they were guests in Lviv.

Marta went in with them to make sure there was no problem with the reservations. "We'll be back in an hour," she said. "You'll want to bathe and change after a night on the train."

Their rooms were at separate ends of a long corridor. Wolfi insisted, after Marta left, that these accommodations were not acceptable: Charlie Smith could have crossed the border in the car that met him at Čop; he might even now be in the city. God knew where Healey and Schluessel, Schluessel in all likelihood armed, might be lurking.

Molly attempted to quiet his fears. "Why would any of them be dangerous to me?"

"It is enough that they are dangerous."

"We can ask for rooms closer together," she said. "And there is another thing." She told him everything, and it was really very little, that Olia Alexander had said about the man who was, clearly, Bogdan Soltan, the helpful driver and paleoanthropologist: he was the image of a man who'd been a menial but brutal collaborator with a surname different from his presumed father.

Wolfi proposed several innocent explanations for that, of which coincidence was the most likely. "And even if they are related," he said, "the older man might have changed his name before the son was born, or in his infancy. His mother might have left the brutish husband and assumed her maiden name, or remarried. He might have been born out of wedlock or orphaned by the war and adopted . . ."

Molly agreed, and told him Nick had made similar suggestions to the housekeeper, who'd been uncharacteristically adamant about her intuition. "Olia's perceptive, I think," she said. "I'd like to know more about Bogdan. And, if Healey's diagrams are meant to correspond with pictures of Tuttle and the Ukrainians—like the Last Supper, there were thirteen at table, Tuttle and the twelve constitution-drafters—I'm almost positive that the notation for him was different from Marta's."

Molly had done her best to memorize the diagram; there were circles where heads might be and the circle at Tuttle's place was empty; the other twelve were marked with one of three arithmetical signs, $<$, $>$, and $=$, less than, more than, or equal to some quantity. Marta, or the circle to the right of the empty circle, had definitely been noted as less than whatever it was. Molly could not remember exactly where Bogdan had been sitting, but she thought that his side of the table was marked mostly with equal signs. "How long have you known Marta?" she asked.

"Almost as long as I've known you," he said, and she thought he blushed as he spoke. "We were visiting fellows, she and I, at Oxford, at St. Antony's, in the fall term after the summer I met you in Vienna."

"That was five years ago." Molly remembered it well. "How was she able to travel? She was a well-known dissident, wasn't she?"

"She'd been refused an exit visa several times. Finally they agreed to let her go, if she left her daughter behind."

It was that simple to control people, Molly thought. Scholars may travel if they leave hostages: this practice moderates the views expressed abroad and lessens the likelihood of defection. "The little girl's father was amenable?"

"I don't know much about him and the girl was not so little. Twelve perhaps. She stayed with Marta's sister."

Molly decided not to explore Marta's domestic arrangements. "Wolfi, don't you imagine people escaped from
the city through the sewer pipes, as the Red Army advanced?"

"Certainly. The Black Sea ports were in Soviet hands,
but escaping Nazis had plenty of help, going west and
south, through Romania and Croatia, from local fascists,
from some clergy—"

"From some Americans." Molly felt this shame keenly.
"From our incipient cold warriors."

"Healey's Father Paul might have begun the journey to
America from Lviv?" He understood her meaning. "Of
course. The city would have been an obvious point of
departure. Marta will know these things."

Marta and Bogdan, who arrived ready to conduct a
three-hour walking tour of the city knew, between them,
the answers to almost any question a visitor could pose.
Bogdan, a racy storyteller, took the narrative up through
the Crusades and Marta carried it to the present. They
saw Greek, Armenian, and Byzantine basilicas; a baroque
chapel with a translucent alabaster *Pietà*; the old German
church of St. Mary on Rosa Luxembourg Street; fountains, arsenals, and houses of Renaissance merchants; a
monastery Joseph II had closed and reopened as a prison;
the Museum of Ecumenism, hastily assembled from the
collection of the Museum of Atheism on the eve of the
first visit of the American ambassador to Ukraine; and an
old Hassidic *shul*, now the Museum of Yiddish Culture.

"There was a Reform Synagogue," Marta told them as
they walked through the square in which the building
once stood, "built by enlightened German-speaking Jews
around the time that reform congregations were established in Krakow and Prague. Its rabbi was an important
Galician republican. More conservative Jews regarded
him as a dangerous modernizer and he was poisoned by

a servant during the abortive revolution of 1848. It was thought that reactionaries among his own people had placed the boy in his household."

"Poisoned by one of his own servants?" Molly asked.

"An orphan boy on whom he'd taken pity. Do you think this story suggested a method to Caleb Tuttle's killers?" Her rich, compelling voice faltered. "That question has haunted me. It's such a familiar story here, at least among people who know nineteenth-century history."

"How many of the delegation came from western Ukraine?" Wolfi asked. The brilliant morning had become a grey afternoon, and rain was making the cobblestoned streets and sidewalks slippery; Marta, who dressed smartly, caught her heel between two stones and almost fell.

"We should seek shelter," Bogdan said, steadying her. "We should here descend into a beer cellar. I want you to see the walls." He'd promised to show them fragments of the city's medieval fortifications embedded in existing buildings. Lviv had been encircled in the middle ages by a double moat filled with water from the river, since diverted underground, and large flat stones that once lined the inner moat furnished much of the tavern's atmosphere.

The afternoon had grown chilly as well as wet, and they ordered brandy, which the waiter brought in large glasses accompanied by a sugar bowl and a plate of thinly sliced lemons.

"Of the twelve of us," Marta explained, dipping a lemon slice into the small mound of sugar she'd spooned onto the plate, "three come from the west, Bogdan and I and Kyril, who is, frankly, an apparatchik very fast on his feet. But what can you do? Try it like this." She took a sip of cognac, then sucked on the lemon slice she'd rolled in sugar. "Wolfi?" She prepared a slice for him with her long graceful fingers and Ritter took it from her as one accustomed to the practice. "As I was saying, what can we do? Half the university graduates in Ukraine were party members. If we excluded them all from the new regime, there wouldn't be enough people to answer the telephones in government offices . . ."

"There must be degrees of culpability," Molly suggested. "What does Kyril look like? This is very good," she added, dipping a lemon slice in sugar. The fruit, tart and sweet, cut pleasantly through the heavy liquor.

Marta evidently trusted Bogdan and spoke unguardedly in front of him. "Kyril is dapper, with silvery grey hair and lots of it, worn long and curling round his little ears, rather, I think one says, fay. Kyril's a crashing bore, but harmless."

Molly nodded. She knew where he'd sat, two down on Tuttle's left, an equal sign. Possibly that notation meant no better and no worse than some known quantity.

"He seeks to place himself in the Ministry of Culture in Kiev," Bogdan added, "and to that end is cultivating the right-wingers."

Wolfi wanted to explore some technical questions: could the poison have been administered during the meal? Were dishes handed round or served individually? Did Tuttle eat or drink anything, a special mineral water or herbal tea or some private condiment, that the others did not?

Bogdan and Marta both insisted that nothing was served to or eaten by Tuttle that was not passed to everyone else. Neither thought that he could possibly have been poisoned in the course of the meal they shared.

"What about the next morning? Did everyone go directly from Boston to Washington?" Molly asked.

"I did not," Bogdan admitted. "Two of us were taking the train to New York. I went to the natural history museum where works a colleague who interests himself in neolithic sites in the Urals. My cousin Petro as usual overslept and missed the train, but he got a later one and we travelled to Washington together that night."

Marta laughed and ordered another round of drinks. "A flake, I think you say. For Petro, the main purpose of the American trip was to visit the film archive in the Museum of Modern Art. He adores the historical epic, Sergei Eisenstein and your D.W. Griffith, especially."

"We almost missed the train to Washington," Bogdan said, "watching some long film about your Civil War. But Marta, what about Ivan?" He frowned and passed a heavy hand over his forehead, flattening his glossy pompadour.

Marta looked grave. "Ivan did not go with us to Washington. He is opposed to the Zborodny trial," she explained, "and he did not want to take part in talks about the priest's extradition."

"Where's he from, Crimea?" Ritter guessed.

"Yes, from Sevastopol, and extremely nationalistic." Marta confirmed his suspicion. Many Ukrainians regarded the Crimea as unduly Russified and its politicians had taken to exaggerating their Ukrainian roots.

Molly didn't ask Marta to describe Ivan. She preferred not to reveal that she'd seen a photograph of the group or to broach the subject of Healey's diagram until she and Wolfi were alone with Marta. Olia Alexander had been so emphatic about her mistrust of Bogdan. "Where was this Ivan on Thursday morning?" she asked.

"He told some of us he was going to visit relatives outside of Montreal. He did not arrive in Washington until the next Tuesday, as we were preparing to leave."

"He met us at the airport," Bogdan added.

"That's right," Marta said. "He flew in from Canada and never really reentered the United States. He was waiting for us in the transit lounge."

"That doesn't mean he didn't stay in Boston, or even arrive directly from Boston," Molly said. "Just that he got to the Washington airport before you did and cleared customs."

"You're absolutely right," Bogdan agreed. "But I hope you are not thinking that he was giving the poison to Caleb Tuttle when he was pretending to be in Canada. Ivan is a reactionary, in politics and in religion, but he is a man of honor."

Molly was not sure she should rely on Bogdan's estimate of another man's honor, but she recognized an opportunity to explore the group's divisions: did the delegation fall on any subject into three distinct groups, groups which might be more than, less than, or equal to something Ignatius Healey cared about? "How close are you," she asked, "to agreeing on the main features of the new constitution? What do you disagree about?"

Bogdan and Marta both laughed. "Everything," they said, almost in unison.

"We disagree about economic, political, military educational, religious, and judicial matters and about foreign policy. We disagree about the extent to which we should cooperate with the former Soviet republics and with Europe. We disagree about whether the police should be national, provincial, or municipal. We disagree about the grounds for divorce," Marta said, "and about spelling reform."

"We agree on the flag," Bogdan said. "It must be blue and yellow."

"If the rain has stopped, we can continue. We'll show you a church that illustrates just how divided we are," Marta said. "In the eighteenth century, Joseph II turned it into a library to uplift and enlighten the people. *Volksbildung ist Volksbefreiung.*"

"Popular education is popular liberation," Wolfi said,

echoing the maxim. Marta'd always been the soul of kindness.

"The library was destroyed in 1848," she continued, "in the counterrevolution, and rebuilt as a church by Franz Joseph."

"Who not so many libraries was building," Bogdan said, over his shoulder, as he left the table. He ran up and down the steps that led to the street entrance, moving faster and more lightly than Molly expected, and announced that the rain had stopped and they could proceed.

The church Marta described was close by, a nineteenth-century church, classical in aspiration, on whose pillared porch peasant women sold holy cards and plaster-of-Paris statuettes.

"In 1949," Marta told them, "when the communists in Ukraine were fairly resigned to tolerating the Eastern Orthodox Church, an official of the autocephalous Ukrainian Catholic Church—there are Ukrainians who follow Catholic rites but remain independent of Rome as well as Uniates who see themselves as part of Western Christendom—ceded this church to the Orthodox, believing that Christianity could be preserved here only in its officially sanctioned form."

"But you still have all three?" Molly asked.

Marta gestured with her beautiful hands, as if to say, what do you expect? "Naturally, of course, and a variety of schismatics in each. Well, this man who believed himself a realist was assassinated on the steps of this church days after he relinquished control of it."

"By a man who immediately shot himself," Bogdan added, portentously.

"The mystery remains to this day. Was the killer an outraged believer or someone who feared he'd renege on the bargain, or an agent of the KGB . . . ?" Marta posed these unanswered questions as they made their way, through the old market square, the Rynek, back to the Intourist Hotel.

"Or a person with some score to settle arising out of the war." Wolfi could not help but think this likely.

"We are," Marta summed up, "so divided by religion that we must remain a secular republic. We cannot subsidize or favorise any communion. It would be fatal."

When they reached the hotel, Molly asked Marta if she'd like to come upstairs with her before dinner. They were both somewhat disheveled by wind and rain, and Molly wanted a chance to ask Marta privately about a variety of ways in which her associates might divide into three groups. Marta shut the outer and inner doors of a small dark elevator in which instructions in Ukrainian had been painted over a longer notice in Russian, then pushed a sequence of tarnished buttons to set its rattling machinery in motion.

"The trial of Father Paul raises these church-state issues?" Molly asked.

"Of course. And that's one reason some people hope it never takes place. Here Tuttle was very helpful to us," Marta said. "He let us talk around his table and draw our conclusions. The Orthodox Christians were corrupted by Russian patronage and they turned a blind eye to Stalin's crimes. Faced with other temptations, local Catholics collaborated with the Germans."

Molly supplied the obvious conclusion. "Religion should have nothing to gain from supporting any party line."

"That's right. There must be freedom and toleration but not a single kopek of public funds."

"Did Tuttle get you all to agree on that?" Molly asked, as the elevator stopped at the fifth floor.

"Not all," Marta acknowledged. "Each church has special pleaders who think their case is different. Tuttle said he was still having this argument with some Americans."

"Did he mention any particular American?"

"Not by name," Marta said. "He spoke of journalists with bizarre opinions. With us, Kyril and Ivan believe in separate school systems. And Petro sees the issue as aesthetic. He says the state should subsidize all ritual because it's dramatically satisfying."

"Petro, the film buff?" Molly asked, opening the door to her room.

"Petro, the flake." Marta laughed and took off her raincoat. She removed the hairpins from her chignon and laid them in a neat row on a painted tray on the bed table; sitting on the edge of the bed, she began to brush her hair with hard, quick strokes. "I've long been curious to know you, Molly," she said. "When I first met Wolfi, you were very much on his mind."

Molly, who was standing at the room's small wash basin, coaxing hot water from an inadequate tap, turned round to face her. She had not thought that Wolfi, so courtly and reticent—"Ritter" meant "knight" and the name fit him—would discuss one woman with another.

"He never meant to tell me about you," Marta explained. "He talked about you, and to you, only in his sleep."

CHAPTER

18

A THIRD MAN, the dapper, silver-haired Kyril, was waiting with Ritter and Bogdan Soltan in the hotel lobby. It was Kyril Dobrylko, renowned for his work in the phenomenology of de-Stalinization and actively seeking the presidency of the philosophical section of the Ukrainian Academy of Sciences. When Bogdan introduced him to Molly, Kyril Dobrylko bent low over her hand, then raised it to his lips. "I'm just back from Kiev," he said, breathless with excitement, releasing Molly's hand and kissing Marta on both cheeks.

"Did you run all the way?" Marta asked.

"I should have. I would have. Had I known your friend Ritter was in Lviv. I was just telling him and our dear Bogdan that the Minister's agreed to see Helmut Schluessel."

"The Minister of Culture." Bogdan reminded them that this was the functionary in whom Kyril Dobrylko fixed his hopes. "Let's talk in the car. Kyril knows where we can get petrol."

Molly, collecting her thoughts on a variety of subjects, got into the front seat, next to Bogdan. Kyril took the place previously occupied by the luggage, leaving Ritter and Marta Tsevchenska to share, once again, the scant space in the back of the little Volga. "The evening's fine, after the rain, and we've hours of light left," Marta said. "Can you get us enough petrol to drive out to the castle and back?"

Kyril's comical look conveyed the assurance that he could grant any wish. "Near to my friend's garage lives a woman who sells caviar and strawberries."

"The Minister's agreed to see Schluessel or actually to work with him?" Wolfi was gravely concerned.

"No firm deal, thus far. I advised him against it, but he expects very substantial benefits from cooperating with the filming."

"Filming what?" Molly hadn't heard that Schluessel was making a documentary. She was not surprised, though, that he sought a wider audience for his appalling views.

Wolfi explained, deeply chagrined by the crudity of the tale he had to tell, that Schluessel believed, along with too many of his compatriots, that Jewish interests controlled Hollywood and systematically distorted popular conceptions of the war.

"Wolfi, the America Firsters believed that too. Charles Lindbergh made speeches about it, so did Joe Kennedy— that movies got us into the war."

"And there were many great anti-appeasement films," Marta said. "Remember, we saw *The Lady Vanishes* in Oxford."

"It's worse than that," Wolfi said. "Schluessel insists that the sufferings of the Jews are exaggerated, blown, he says, out of all proportions. He wants to make a movie about the sufferings of ethnic Germans in the East."

"Scores of Germans were killed in Gdansk," Bogdan said.

"Which Schluessel will go to his grave calling Danzig," Wolfi said, interrupting him. "We know Germans were killed in Gdansk and in Poznan on the eve of the invasion. Poles thought they were fifth columnists. No doubt some were. Germans died also in forced deportations after the Russians annexed East Prussia. But all that is morally, categorically different from genocide."

Usually, Molly thought, he speaks of these things more in sorrow than in anger; now he's enraged. "Have you seen the script?" she asked.

"Schluessel shows it only to people he trusts, but word gets around—Jewish commissars rape virginal displaced persons. Basically Jews command the Red Army because Slavs are cretins."

"He'll tone down the anti-Slav bits, if he can film in Ukraine." Kyril Dobrylko did not like to disagree with Cabinet ministers, but this affair made him uneasy. "Petro has volunteered to help with the revisions. He says the project excites him cinematographically. Turn off here," he instructed Bogdan, "and pull into that shed."

Inside the shed, a man was working under the hood of a taxi. He wiped his hands on a towel that hung from his belt and shook hands with Dobrylko, who got out of the car and clapped him on the shoulder. Kyril chatted with him as he filled their tank with gas, checked the oil, and cleaned the windshield with his towel, then climbed back into the car. "He's getting the caviar," he explained, as the man left the shed through a back door. "His son entered the Polytechnical School last year after I had a word with the admissions director."

"Petro's not serious?" Marta objected. "He can't really be willing to help Schluessel?"

"Who knows when Petro's serious? But the Minister feels under great pressure to decide. You're an American." Kyril addressed Molly. "What's the meaning of the expression 'hot to trot'?"

"Eager to make a deal, to get on with some project."

"That's what I thought it must mean," Kyril said. "The Minister prides himself on knowing American slang. The Croatians, he told me, are hot to trot. We'll lose the project if we don't act fast."

Wolfi erupted. "God in Heaven, the Croatians, our grateful protégés."

"*Plus ça change.*" Marta laid an affectionate and restraining hand on his arm. "They'll never change. Don't take it so hard, Wolfi. Some things will never change."

The enterprising taxi driver returned with strawberries, peaches, and caviar; he took several bottles of vodka out of the trunk of his cab and, accepting payment only for the strawberries, which a neighbor had grown, directed them to a farm down the road where bread was baked daily.

A COPPER SUN hung low over the fields, casting long shadows: three more nights until midsummer's night, and the sun hovered motionless, unwilling to set, charging every leaf and blade of grass with a seemingly inextinguishable light. The hilltops shone, the pastures glowed. Molly found it almost impossible to reconcile this vision of abiding beauty with her knowledge of the events that had taken place nearby.

"On that hillside," Marta said, "was a camp for Russian POWs. Those who did not die of starvation and exposure during the winter were shot in the spring, while the ammunition lasted, at any rate. Italian soldiers too."

"Why Italians?" Molly asked. "Was there a mutiny?" She thought a refusal to fight for Hitler spoke well of the men.

"Not precisely a mutiny. After the king of Italy surrendered to the allies, Italian soldiers asked to be sent home. They were told they could go if they left their arms."

"But"—Bogdan finished Marta's story—"as soon as the poor devils disarmed themselves, they were shot."

"Well," Marta said briskly. She had the historian's ability to imagine herself in another's place. "It would have been awkward to release soldiers with firsthand knowledge that the eastern front was collapsing."

"Look, Molly, there's the castle," Bogdan said. As he drove he grew more animated. "Is it not beautiful?" He stopped, put the car into first gear, and began cautiously to ascend the steep, narrow, pebble-strewn road that led to the castle.

Another group of sightseers was starting down the road on foot, and Molly thought she recognized someone among the stragglers who remained on the summit, reluctant to leave the splendid ruin. "May I?" Bogdan kept a pair of binoculars in an open compartment under the dashboard.

"Please," he said, which meant "help yourself," and "as you wish."

A figure stood midway up a stone staircase that wound around the crumbling tower, shielding its eyes from the sun's slanting rays, surveying the hilly expanse of land between the castle and the western horizon. Molly focussed the glasses and made sure.

Ritter asked her what she was looking at and she handed him the glasses. "The boy we saw at Čop."

Charlie Smith climbed the remaining steps, casting long glances at the surrounding hills and fields. When he reached the top, he threw out his chest, lifted his chin, and folded his arms, as if in secure and triumphant possession. "This castle belongs to whom?" Molly asked.

"To the state," Kyril Dobrylko said. "We plan to use it as a conference center. It's a picturesque site, and the outbuildings can be fitted up as guesthouses. The banquet hall is splendid, and we'll put racquetball courts and a sauna in the keep."

"It will be very comfortable." Bogdan parked the car close to the castle gate. "I hope every year we schedule many events for anthropologists."

"Baron Charlie," Ritter said softly, handing the glasses back to Molly and walking with her under the portcullis and into the castle courtyard. "He looks as though he bought whatever story he was told."

"Anyone could point him to a castle and tell him it would be his one day," Molly said. "But he's actually here, and someone took some trouble to get him here."

"I can think of many bad reasons to do that, and no good ones. Who do you suppose Mr. Barbarossa was, who called Charlie this spring? And did Nick not say that Ignatius Healey had tried to reach him also?"

"Should I talk to Charlie, do you think? Tell him that through a funny coincidence I know his family, and they're worried and he should call them."

"No," he said. "Whatever he's doing here will be foolish or dangerous, most likely both. He must know nothing about you. He should not even hear us speak English." He called to the others, in German, to join them.

A voice outside the gate presently called to Charlie, as "Karl," and the youth, after some minutes, made his way down the hill, stopping often and looking back, enraptured, at the castle of his dreams.

MARTA PRESIDED over a sybaritic picnic: caviar and strawberries were surprisingly good together; coarse bread, fresh white cheese, and perfect peaches even better. The vodka was a Polish variety, headily aromatic, scented with a grass upon which the few remaining, greatly endangered and carefully protected Eurasian bison were said to graze. "These cannot be hunted," Wolfi remarked, looking at the bison silhouette on the label.

"You can see them, though," Marta said. "In a Polish national forest on the Russian frontier. You might have time after you go to Krakow."

"Isn't there a national forest between Lviv and Krakow?" Molly asked.

"Yes," Bogdan said, "Hunting is permitted year-round because the flora and fauna are not so rare. I can drive you through it, if you want to go to Krakow by car . . . and if Kyril can get petrol."

"No problem," that resourceful person assured them.

"It's good of you," Molly said. Bogdan appeared a fine fellow, but she wanted to talk this offer over with Wolfi.

"Can we let you know in the morning?" Ritter sensed her hesitation.

"Of course, you will want to sleep on the idea," Kyril said urbanely. "An hour's notice will locate all the gas you need."

CHAPTER

$\boxed{19}$

Nick Hannibal watched as two young women in orange smocks numbered the bricks that were about to be removed from the wall of Caleb Tuttle's cellar. Masons waited to begin their task, kidding with police officers about the care the girls were lavishing on the wall. Lottie Parsons from the Commonwealth Landmarks Commission checked the numbering, took a few additional Polaroid pictures, then turned to confer with Nick.

"It would be better, I think, to begin from the left side," she said. "If that poses no problem for you, Lieutenant. The mortar looks weaker there, and we can minimize the damage to the supporting walls, if we keep the banging and chipping to a, well, to a minimum."

"Whatever you prefer." Nick had found several loose bricks himself on a previous visit; he'd removed them, shone a flashlight into the tunnel, and satisfied himself that the objects shoved through the wall had been discarded, not cached. No wire or twine had been attached to haul things back through the holes in the wall, and nothing had fallen close enough to be retrieved by hand. "Start any place you like." He found Lottie Parsons easy to work with: intent on her own task, but recognizing that a murder investigation might take precedence.

They were both eager to see what lay behind the wall. Lottie Parsons hoped it had been bricked over in haste and some terrific slave diary or carving or artifact overlooked. Nick wanted to find something, anything, that might clarify the progress of the barium-based pesticide from the garage or wine cellar into the salad Tuttle ate, and possibly shared with Ignatius Healey, on the day before he died.

The masons removed the bricks singly, taking care that none fell into the tunnel to crush or disarrange whatever lay behind the wall; they handed the bricks to the women, who wrapped each one in canvas and stacked them in piles of ten. It was slow going. Jimmy Sabatini came in from the garden every half hour or so to talk with the cops and check out the girls, summer interns at the Landmarks Commission, art history majors with good legs, tanned from tennis and slightly bowed from riding. One of them, living with a law student, met Jimmy's gaze with a direct, inviting smile. The other avoided his glance and cast a more maidenly eye on Nick Hannibal. The planes of the detective's face were marvelous, she thought, as was the tension of his body in repose. She was serious about sculpture, but her analysis grew less formal as she watched him wait, curbing his impatience but just barely, while the wall came down.

Lights, like klieg lights, had been put in place; Nick switched them on and stepped, at last, into the tunnel. "Vinegar bottle," he shouted triumphantly. "Maps, too. We'd better take some pictures first."

"Leave everything *in situ*, okay?" Ms. Parsons said.

The police photographers took about twenty minutes; Lottie Parsons took ten minutes more, recording the scene from other vantage points. When she finished, Nick picked up the lower half of a brown glass bottle: it was the same brand of imported balsamic vinegar he'd taken from Caleb Tuttle's kitchen. The bottle had shattered when it was pushed or thrown into the tunnel and none of the liquid remained. The vinegar had seeped, he imagined, into the tunnel's dirt floor; possibly it had been emptied into a sink, or into the cellar's stationary tubs, before the bottle was ditched. Nonetheless, a white residue clung to the glass, and he could still catch the faint sweet smell of Modena vinegar.

This, he thought, is it. The bottles were switched and a salad made with poisoned vinegar. After the meal, a fresh bottle, or an old bottle previously withdrawn, was put back in place of this one. "This is going to take a while," he told Lottie Parsons. There were papers too—maps, magazines, and a flexible plastic three-ring binder—he decided to leave them until they'd found every fragment of glass.

"I'll stay," she said. "In case something of antiquarian interest turns up. Nan and Liza can go." Nan and Liza reluctantly left, and she settled herself on the horsehair sofa.

The earthen floor of the tunnel was combed for brown glass, and during the search Nick mulled over a number of possibilities: Caleb Tuttle almost certainly ate salad at lunch or dinner on the last day of his life. Mrs. Alexander had left him lettuce, washed and wrapped in linen towels, and found the towels in the pantry when she returned. If Tuttle ate the lettuce late in the day, and perhaps made the dressing himself, who removed the poisoned vinegar? Daphne Robbins and Jimmy Sabatini, who seemed to find the cellar a congenial place, admitted they had been alone in the house, alone except for her very young children and Tuttle himself, most of Thursday night and all Friday morning. He had not asked either of them if they'd gone to the cellar during this period. He wanted that question to come as a surprise.

Charlie Smith, Nick felt this hunch pretty strongly, had spent some time here, but he could have stayed unbeknownst to the two of them. Neither was observant, and Jimmy admitted to drinking heavily Thursday evening. On the other hand, maybe he'd had less booze and less action than he claimed and done worse things. Possibly, Nick thought, but unlikely.

Jimmy had said, and Daphne'd confirmed this, that Tuttle had not been up and around Thursday afternoon. He could have gone out and come back unnoticed—or unnoticed by two people with little interest in his comings and goings—or he could have prolonged his afternoon nap because he already felt unwell.

That seemed likely and raised a more complicated problem. If Tuttle had eaten the salad at lunch, had the salad been offered to Healey too? Offered and declined? No, Nick thought, offered and accepted, but just lettuce, no salad dressing. Healey was overweight and something of a fop, quite possibly the sort who drank diet soda but never skipped dessert. This idea appealed to Nick, who ate anything he wanted whenever he had time, and it raised, logically, two more possibilities: either Healey knew the vinaigrette was poisoned and had a pretext for declining it—trying to stay fit—or he did not know and the killer took a hell of a chance.

Tuttle's death had appeared natural and his murder would, but for his altruism, have gone undetected. If Healey had died too—or even developed symptoms for which he'd sought treatment—crime would have been apparent from the start. These ideas were tentative, Nick recognized, but they suggested that Healey killed Tuttle himself or that another killer had been extremely reckless or extremely lucky. A third possibility, implausible but not impossible, was this: the killer possessed certain knowledge of Healey's social engagements and dietary eccentricities.

"Lieutenant, I've got the bottlecap." A patrolman spotted the cap, which had rolled, still attached to the broken neck of the bottle, some distance down the tunnel.

"Good job," Nick said. "That looks like all the glass. Take it back to the lab. I want to go through the papers."

Lottie Parsons, who'd been sitting quietly, asked whether she could now explore the tunnel herself. "I won't go too far," she promised. "The walls are bricked for only a few yards, and the supporting timbers in the rest of the tunnel were taken down sixty years ago, but I'm dying to have a look."

"Watch it, lady," one of the masons advised. "There'll be rats."

"Oh, heavens, I don't mind rats," she said. "Would you like to see some nineteenth-century masonry?"

He declined, but Nick said he'd be curious himself, after he looked through the papers. He gathered them up and carried them out into the cellar proper, then laid them on the newly swept floor. There were maps of Eastern Europe, including a large scale German ordinance map of the environs of Lemberg with an area outlined in blue magic marker; several copies of the magazine for mercenaries, *Soldier of Fortune*, with no address label, bought presumably at newsstands; and the swimsuit issue of *Sports Illustrated*, borrowed presumably from the subscriber, Thomas J. Smith, Jr. Next, he took up the three-ring binder and began to read its contents.

"I didn't see any live rats"—Lottie Parsons emerged from the tunnel—"but I saw a rat's nest. At first I thought this was another dead one, but it's a rabbit's foot. They stash things, you know, rats, lots of rodents do."

A cool lady, Nick thought. The charm was made from

a long, brown foot, darker and larger than domestic hares, an animal like the ones the Smiths raised. "Very interesting," he said. "Thank you. And let's collect the rats," he directed two of his crew, "to see if they drank any pesticide."

"It's modern," she said sadly, handing Nick the rabbit's foot. "I hoped when I saw what it was that it had some connection with voodoo. One always wants to know how fugitive slaves sustained themselves, the spiritual resources they drew upon. But I'm afraid this foot's pretty fresh."

"I'd say so and not very spiritual, but a big help to me. I need to talk to the woman in the third-floor apartment, Ms. Parsons," he said. "I'll leave some men, if you want to stay in the cellar."

"I'm all set for now, thanks. Will you be working late? Would you like dinner at some point?"

He told her he would not have time; they were short-handed now that the vacation season had begun.

DAPHNE ROBBINS sensed that the detective didn't like her. He was perfectly polite; in fact, rather nicer to her than any of her former boyfriends or her husband's professedly sensitive divinity-school crowd. Nonetheless, she knew he disapproved of her. He must have guessed about her and Jimmy. This cop was drop-dead good-looking, no reason he shouldn't be choosy. She'd seen him in the garden a week ago with a woman; they'd moved and talked together as though they got along very well. He wasn't wearing a wedding ring and she thought cops generally did if they were married, but this one did not look unattached.

Today, he'd come with another woman: that snotty bitch preservationist, an aging art-history type for whom the really creative women, the performing artists she'd known, had nothing but contempt. They'd gone into the cellar together to open up the old tunnel. Swell. They wouldn't find anything there that would cause her any trouble.

The detective seemed to enjoy the company of that sort of quick, purposeful woman. Daphne was more laid back. She didn't see the point of exerting herself; things came to her—like Jimmy. He wasn't as smooth as the detective, but he was cuter, raunchier, and she liked the way he flaunted his sex. She kidded him about putting his best crotch forward. The detective was more subtle. He'd be good, she thought, but she didn't need refinement. Jimmy's enthusiasm suited her. You didn't need the whole fucking *Kama Sutra* . . .

So, when Nick Hannibal knocked on her door and interrupted her train of thought she repeated aloud, "You don't need the whole fucking *Kama Sutra*."

"I've come about something else altogether," he said. "Is this your handwriting?" The writing in the margins of the script he'd found in the three-ring binder looked like penmanship he'd seen in Scattergood College examination bluebooks on Molly's desk. From time to time she read him amusing passages from these books, and the funniest mistakes were usually set down in that looping, slanted, boarding-school hand.

"Yeah," Daphne said. "It's a crappy script. It reads like a lousy translation."

Nick had made the same judgment; he'd also remembered Jimmy's asking whether Charlie Smith was really going to be a movie star.

"But you coached Charlie, didn't you? You made these notes for him?"

"He was clueless," she said. "He can barely read, let alone act. I had to write foreign place names out for him phonetically, and even then he stumbled over them."

"He was here, wasn't he, the week Tuttle died, when his family thought he was missing?"

"Yeah," she said. "But he's a big boy. If he doesn't want to go home, I'm not going to make him." Her children were napping and she felt tired. "Can we talk another time?" she said. "The bigger I get, the worse I feel and I want to lie down."

"I'm sorry." They'd been standing at the door and she had not invited him in. He regretted that he'd been inconsiderate, but her manner did not encourage solicitude. "Could you give me another few minutes, if we sat down?"

She let him in and stretched out on the couch. He sat opposite her in a frayed armchair.

"How did he get hold of this play? Did he tell you?" Could one of Charlie's skinhead friends have literary aspirations? Angry young skinheads? The work was painfully amateur, yet beautifully printed: a clean photocopy of what looked to be a laser-printed original. Moreover, the spelling and punctuation were faultless. Nick had read enough reports written by rookie cops, with considerably more education than Charlie's pals were likely to have among them, to recognize this as unusual. Kids with associate's and bachelor's degrees in criminal justice mixed up "whose" and "who's," and "they're" and "their" and "there." He proofread his subordinates' reports these days, after losing convictions because of their incoherence; but this text was, if anything, clear, and any number of exotic place names—above which Daphne had written the simplest phonetic version—appeared to be spelled correctly.

"It's not a play. It's a movie script. These are camera notes, not stage directions," she showed him. " 'POV' stands for 'Point-of-View,' " she said, rubbing her left breast. "My boobs are sore," she explained. "Look, Charlie's a stupid little shit. I helped him because Jimmy asked me to. The script is crap, and there will be bobsleds in hell before a movie like this gets produced. Who's going to make it, Woody Allen?"

"But you don't know who wrote it, or how Charlie got hold of it?"

"No," she said. "I didn't care and didn't ask. I'm sorry." Maybe she should have talked to Charlie about how god-awful it was, but he was so dumb it didn't matter what he thought. "I'm sorry," she repeated.

"Don't worry about it," Nick said. "Get some rest."

NICK READ the script from beginning to end that night, eating hamburgers at his desk. The story was coarse and derivative, its best sequence stolen from *Ivanhoe*, with Scott's tolerationist point blunted: the maiden ready to hurl herself from a castle tower to escape a fate worse than death was a peasant's, not a merchant's, daughter, and the would-be rapist a moneylender, not a Crusader. A crowd scene followed in which angry villagers took horrific vengeance on the lecherous Jew. Around midnight, Nick left a message for the hate-crimes unit—they worked a regular eight-hour day—asking them for the name of their contact at the Anti-Defamation League.

CHAPTER

20

"THE WHOLE countryside seems to be surrendering," Molly said, as the car bounced along a badly rutted road. White flags fluttered low over the sown fields.

"The peasants believe these flags frighten the boars away from their seedlings. This belief comforts the farmers." Bogdan Soltan chuckled low in his throat. "I think it presents no problem for the boars."

Molly and Wolfgang Ritter had accepted his offer to drive them to Krakow. That had been settled the previous morning when Marta stopped by their hotel to see if either of them wanted to go for a walk. Molly did and Ritter, trusting her instincts, said he'd catch up with them later at the University.

"My office is in the main building"—Marta had given good directions—"across from Franko Park. Oh, Molly," she'd said with a laugh, "not what you're thinking. Ivan Franko, with a 'k,' was a Ukrainian national hero, a romantic poet with socialist leanings, from a generation when decent people *were* socialists. That's why the communists were willing to put up a great vulgar socialist realist statue of him, looking from a distance like Lenin."

As they'd walked through the city, admiring art deco facades and Renaissance fountains, Molly was determined, first, to make plain that she and Wolfi did not sleep jointly on any topic and, second, to learn more about Bogdan.

"So, Tuttle's housekeeper recognized him as his father's son?" Marta had said. "What an amazing memory she must have. Soltan is the family's real name. The other name was a *nom de guerre*. Bogdan's father was a double agent, from a proletarian background which he exaggerated. Germans would talk in his presence as if they were alone, as if he were a dog or a piece of furniture. I knew him," she'd said. "He died only a few years ago."

"You trust Bogdan completely?"

Marta had sighed. "I trust him completely and I like him very much."

But not as much as she likes another, Molly had thought and urged her to come to Krakow with them. That was impossible. Marta's daughter played the flute in a student orchestra and the orchestra was performing the Mozart flute concerto in Yalta that weekend. "Bogdan's fond of my daughter," she'd added.

THEY HAD been driving for hours on roads that seemed centuries older than the superhighway that linked Vienna and Budapest, stopping from time to time to admire the naive art in village churches. They passed, too, many abandoned towns.

"These old *shtetls* are so sad," Bogdan said, as they approached another, a collection of ramshackle huts. "This is Zborodny. The shops and the high school were razed, and the houses plundered. After the massacre, no one returned."

"I'd like to get out," Ritter said.

"Certainly, my friend. But you will find nothing."

Molly and Bogdan walked with him, Molly holding his hand, down the dirt road that had been the main street. Grass grew between the few paving stones that remained. Most of the stones had been taken up after the war and used elsewhere for rebuilding. Only the cracked stones had been left behind.

"There are not even any animals," Wolfi said. "It is completely lifeless, except for the grass." He continued to walk until he reached a pile of stones by the side of the road. "Why were these stones not taken?" he asked.

"The peasants are superstitious," Bogdan explained. "This heap would have formed the base of a shrine, and the people will not steal from the Holy Virgin."

"Yes, of course, I remember."

"You remember, Wolfi?" Molly asked.

"My father wrote to my mother about these customs." He held her hand more tightly. "I am so grateful you are here with me."

There was nothing more to see in Zborodny. The bodies had been removed from the mass grave the previous summer and reinterred in Israel. Grass grew on that site also, and some wildflowers.

"Come," Molly said. "We can do nothing here." They walked in silence back to the car, passing another heap of stones as they left the corpse of the town.

Patches of forest came closer together now, between the plowed fields, and they soon entered the park that extended past the frontier and into Poland. The gate-keeper on the Ukrainian side told them a shooting party of Germans had arrived earlier that morning. "Drive safely," he said, "and keep your heads down. They look like rich fools." He waved them into the deep forest, where groves of white birch trees relieved the sombre darkness. They saw a few red deer, and once a small and timid boar watched them from the middle of the road and then scampered—Molly had never seen a piglike animal move so quickly or so charmingly—into hiding among the trees. An hour later they emerged from the forest, into the fields of southeastern Poland.

In these fields, aged women toiled with scythes and rakes cutting hay for the same giant haystacks they'd seen from the train. Molly asked Bogdan about them.

"Nasty, aren't they?" he said. "People used to be impaled on them in peasant revolts."

"How recently?" Ritter asked. "Collaborators too?" He'd said scarcely a word since they'd left Zborodny.

"Maybe a few. Rough justice tends to be traditional and here in the borders little has changed. There was great resistance to collectivization," he said, turning the conversation tactfully to farming methods, "and small-holding farmers cannot afford machinery. Look." He stopped the car. "That's the most mechanization you'll see."

An old horse pulled a cart across a field; a bent pitchfork lashed to the rear axle gathered some portion of the mown grass over which the cart passed. Periodically, a small boy walking beside the horse stopped and tossed the grass into the cart.

"We have seen very few carts," Wolfi observed, "with or without attachments." He seemed to be making an effort to behave like an ordinary tourist seeing a country for the first time.

"I haven't even seen a wheelbarrow," Molly said. Old women, and they did seem to be withered crones, wrinkled and toothless—sprightly youths and graceful damsels were not mowing in Poland—cut a patch of grass and carried it in their arms, usually an inconvenient distance, to the thorny poles on which the hay would dry.

"People don't worry about how hard the old women

work," Bogdan explained. "You may see some sledges with wooden runners or flat wagons with long poles that can be pulled by people or mules. Farming's very primitive here. As we go west, closer to Krakow, people are more prosperous."

And they saw, presently, substantial three-story houses under construction. Huge barns and granaries rose close to the houses; and although there were many old churches, new ones seemed to spring up every hundred yards. "People work abroad for a year and return with enough money to house their entire extended family," Bogdan said. "Also relatives abroad send money. Agriculture improves, and in industrial pollution"—he pointed to an ochre cloud on the horizon—"Poland can match any country in the world."

Factories in Nowa Huta, the new town built in the fifties to outrage and subdue Krakow, continued to spew filth over the old city that had been so hostile to the communists. Krakow seemed, apart from its brown air in which particulate emissions hung suspended, like a medieval city. Unlike Lviv's market square, Krakow's Rynek had stalls for merchants and a timbered Rathaus. Eighteenth-century palais and baroque churches dotted the side streets, but the main buildings, the cathedral and the Jagiellonian University, were unchanged since the days of Copernicus.

The conference they had come for would begin the next day. Today they would see the city and tomorrow retrace their route, eastward, towards the summer palace of one of the prince-primates of Galicia, an elector of the Holy Roman Empire, which had already been converted into a conference center. Bogdan was staying in Krakow with his cousin Petro who was filming a pilot for a BBC series on the life of the great astronomer; but, always dependable, he promised to drive them to the conference in the morning. "We'll pick up that parcel tomorrow morning," he said to Ritter, "when I come to collect your luggage."

Molly wanted to see the Czartorysky collection, paintings belonging to a Polish princely family of unparalleled taste, exhibited in their Krakow palais. They had amassed a remarkable store, the best, Leonardo da Vinci's *Lady with an Ermine*, whose long, white, nervous fingers held the equally long white body of an animal whose limbs displayed a musculature more complex than the lady's.

"Finer, don't you think, than the *Mona Lisa*?" Wolfi asked her.

"Much finer, and better than the *Ginevra da Benci* in Washington. It's my favorite da Vinci, oh . . ."

They stood silent before an empty space on the adjoining wall. No attempt had been made to erase the injury or make good the loss. A small white card gave witness in French, which Molly suspected the Czartoryskys spoke better than they spoke Polish, that Raphael's portrait of a young man had been "pillaged by the Germans."

"French is always candid," Wolfi said. "Have you noticed that other memorials in the city speak of victims or heroes of the 'Hitlerite' invasion?"

"I have." 'Hitlerite' had usually been the only word she'd recognized in the inscription. The necessity to accept East Germans as brothers in the Warsaw Pact had, it seemed, cast remembrance in ideological rather than national terms. "Let's get some coffee. The guidebook says there's a coffeehouse near here with *fin de siècle* stained glass."

They found it easily—it was full of disputatious students in blue jeans and extras from the Copernicus film in more gorgeous academic costume—and settled into a purple plush booth of almost Viennese opulence. The Turkish coffee they ordered came in tall glasses and looked like the city's air: particles in suspension. They watched them settle, then sipped the coffee. "It has a kind of gritty integrity," Molly said. "It certainly tastes like coffee."

A pastry cart sped by them, summoned imperiously by a man at a large table in the back of the shop. Ignatius Healey was in Krakow and in his element. "Marvelous, I'll have one of everything, except the napoleons. I hate usurpers."

The seminarians surrounding him tittered, and one ventured to say, "We had hopes of Bonaparte, at one time. He promised an independent Poland."

The youths peppered him with questions, admiring and deferential at first, more pointed as they took his measure. Molly, who'd read Healey's mesmerizingly frightful column for years, ignored him. Wolfi, less familiar with his views, eavesdropped openly. Molly couldn't blame him: another country's lunatic fringe might actually comfort Wolfi, and Healey was in rare form.

"He who says 'sin is not crime,' " Healey was saying, "is sending a not-so-subtle message that sin does not matter—that evil is a matter of indifference to the state."

The pastry cart returned and Haley browsed more selectively, choosing raspberry tarts and miniature cheesecakes called *serki*. "Voluntary prayer"—he choked with mock indignation and cheesecake crumbs—"one might as well endorse voluntary monogamy. You will find the same people in favor of both."

"Nobody's volunteered for monogamy with him," Molly whispered across the table.

Ignatius Healey gave a long instruction, which one of the students translated for a waiter, who returned, after some minutes, with brandy and sliced lemons. Healey unwrapped a number of sugar lumps and carefully crushed them with the back of a spoon. "The only purpose for which I use sugar," he confided to the youths who watched the process curiously. "I use artificial sweeteners for coffee, but it's a most inadequate substitute with brandy." He took up a thin slice of lemon with a fork and covered it with pulverized sugar. Marta's long fingers had rolled the thinly sliced lemon like a cigarette; Healey's fat pink hands plied the utensils with an almost sacramental solemnity, and Molly wondered who had introduced him to this practice. A Polish boy raised that question. "Do all Americans drink brandy like that?"

"Gracious, no," Healey said. "My countrymen have no time for elegance. They fail to comprehend the beauty and indeed the utility of ceremony. Separation of church and state," he fulminated, "anomie, lawlessness, where medieval Christendom had forged the Great Chain of Being, modern man hurtles among self-seeking atoms driven by appetite—"

"What about the Invisible Hand?" a robust young man asked. "Is not some order created *wolens-nolens*?" A seminarian, he used the Latin form of "willy-nilly," and he liked Adam Smith very much. The Scotsman was more profound, he thought, than the Nobel Laureate, Professor Dr. Milton Friedman, and a finer English prose stylist than Professor Dr. Paul Samuelson.

"The economy may be fruitfully viewed in that fashion, though Smith is no less depraved, *au fond*, than any other eighteenth-century writer. We shall speak of this again," Healey said. "Perhaps tomorrow evening, after the first session of the conference."

CHAPTER

21

Ritter AND the other organizers of the conference on the Reformation and Counter-Reformation in the East had assembled a mixed and illustrious crowd. The throng did justice to the setting, an Elector's summer palace with extensive gardens that mingled on all sides with the surrounding farms. Gervase Wattle of All Souls' recalled Gerard Manley Hopkins on Oxford's vanished power, " 'Rural rural keeping—folk, flock, and flower.' " Molly thought the place did look untroubled by the importunities of reform and rebellion.

Academics were arriving from Western Europe and from North America and hastening, singly and in groups, to the opening reception, where the Eastern Europeans had already gathered. Molly met Ivan Vorenchuk from Sevastopol. She recognized him as the man who'd sat next to Kyril at Caleb Tuttle's table; Molly could not remember the sign that marked his place, but she was fairly sure he'd been more than or less than whatever was wanted, not a matter of indifference.

She was talking with Vorenchuk, who struck her as active, principled and ruthless, when Helmut Schluessel interrupted them. He had not been invited, he acknowledged; he worked on a later period, but he was vacationing in the area and he hoped to see some of his old friends. Molly left them in the ballroom and walked out into the garden; when she reentered the room Ivan Vorenchuk had detached himself from Schluessel and was deep in conversation with a Dominican priest from Montreal. He did appear to have Canadian acquaintances.

Ignatius Healey came late, surrounded by a flock of black-robed seminarians, and sought out Molly directly. She could not fight her way clear of him and struggled instead to keep the conversation civil. Art seemed a safe subject and she spoke of the Czartorysky collection and its fabulous da Vinci.

"In the room with the pilfered Raphael." Healey had admired it earlier in the day.

"Yes, isn't that strange?" she said. "Who would steal anything but the da Vinci? How good could the Raphael possibly have been?"

"In your innocence, my dear," Healey said, "you ignore the subject of the painting, a beautiful boy. It likely reminded some German officer of his orderly."

Wolfi was talking with Gervase Wattle, across the room from them and a good distance from Schluessel, who, she thought, had thus far not seen him. Molly wasn't sure how far Healey's voice had carried. Evidently too far, for Wattle instantly remarked in his light dismissive English voice that could be heard for miles and brooked no argument, "The most rabid fag bashers, don't you know, Ritter, are all bent themselves."

Molly joined them and asked to be introduced to Wattle, whose work she greatly admired.

"Don't worry, Molly." Ritter drew her hand through his arm and held it for a long minute. "Schluessel brings out the worst in me, but I won't embarrass you again."

* * *

AFTER THE reception, which prolonged itself into a sumptuous buffet, the assemblage dispersed, some to the library, some to the garden, some back to their rooms, austere but comfortable cells in the former cloister where they could revise or finish or begin their papers for the next day's sessions.

Ignatius Healey had gathered a group of young people, mostly seminarians, around him on the terrace that led from the ballroom into the formal garden. Molly and Wolfi were walking with Bogdan Soltan and Gervase Wattle among the topiary, catching snatches of Healey's homily.

"In the realm of family and society, hierarchy is natural." He could elaborate on this theme for hours.

"If hierarchy is natural, why must we legislate it?" The young man who admired Adam Smith had been captivated by the idea of liberty.

"We must nurture order and support it, not undermine it," Healey said. "For example, I have some thoughts on a constitution for Poland, suggested to me by my mentor, Paul Szlepensky, a loyal son of Poland and subject, albeit in exile, of *Maria, Regina Poloniae*. 'Pavlus,' he told me his mother enjoined him as he bade her farewell, 'remember always you are a Pole.' "

Molly hadn't heard Father Paùl's plans for Poland. Others seemed to share her curiosity and several people joined the group around Healey. Half the people present, Molly thought, had written or would be writing constitutions for newly independent countries. Bogdan Soltan smiled in anticipation: Healey struck him as wildly ridiculous and he loved broad comedy.

Healey's, or Paul's, ruminations emerged as fairly standard criticisms of parliamentary democracy. The Western Europeans had heard them, or swatted them up for examinations in political theory, and one by one they drifted away, Wattle alone remaining.

"A bicameral parliament, for example, is inherently flawed. Dualism breeds cynicism. The perfect number, you all recognize to be three."

"Three estates?" Gervase Wattle was disdainful. "My dear fellow, it's been tried. It was called feudalism."

"Three chambers? The deputies we have already make more speeches than we have time to read." Several of the less speculative Poles retired to the bar.

"So, how would you organize the three chambers?" Ivan Vorenchuk asked. Feudalism was not necessarily a bad thing in his mind.

"The lower house would be elected by producers, that is, workers, peasants, and mothers."

"What about fathers?" a shy young woman asked. She was a Hungarian musicologist, interested in Calvin's views on congregational singing.

"A father's biological connection with his child is fleeting," Healey said. "Physical paternity means very little. '*Ignatiku*,' my teacher would often say to me, 'priests are the true fathers of all Christian children.' "

Molly heard this with interest. No biographical sketch of Healey said much about his father.

"And women who are not mothers will have no vote?" the same gentle voice posed this question respectfully.

"Women require grounding in reality," Healey explained. "Else their opinions lack substance, and can have, thus, no consequence."

"Do mothers get multiple votes?" Bogdan was entering into the spirit of the discussion. "One vote per child? Can women vote as soon as they conceive, when the fetus is viable, or only after delivery?"

Healey ignored these questions, which he felt to be unserious. "An upper house would be composed of professionals and men of letters, the learned laity. I see no reason to exclude women who have qualified as lawyers or doctors."

"Magnanimous," Wolfi said. He and Molly were sitting on a marble bench on the edge of the terrace. "This is odd though, something about what he's saying is odd."

"Everything about this is odd," Molly said.

"Lastly, informing and harmonising relations between the mass of the people and the secular elites," Healey concluded, "the chamber of the clergy."

Healey's audience had dwindled. Bogdan had left; he'd promised to help Petro's film crew early next morning. Wattle was dozing. Ivan Vorenchuk remained and a tall figure Molly thought might be Schluessel, and a smattering of others. It was the seminarian interested in economics who asked whether the clergy of all faiths would be represented.

"Poland is a Catholic nation, is it not? How many Protestants and Jews have you left?"

"Not very many." The boy's voice was hushed with tragedy. "Very few."

"The Holy Spirit has winnowed the fields of Poland. Father Paul made that clear to me. He has threshed the rich, fructifying seed of the true faith from the dry husk of the old covenant and the chaff of dissent. The withered grass has been burned by His fiery breath, and the new grass will spring up, fresh and green."

"The Holy Spirit has done this?" The boy's ruddy face was white above his black soutane. "You speak of the death of millions of men and women? of children? of babies?"

"My spiritual father believes that and I believe it."

"A priest taught you this?"

" 'God has cleansed Poland, *Ignatiku.*' I can hear him say it."

The boy rose unsteadily to his feet and crossed himself. "May God forgive you both."

Healey saw that most of his listeners had left. He took a bottle of brandy from the tray that had been left on the terrace and retired.

Molly and Wolfi sat, side by side, mutually appalled, sharing each other's horror. "We saw the grass at Zborodny," he said.

"Let's walk awhile." Molly could not sit still.

It was midsummer night and the sky was white with no stars visible in it. Daylight had not yet effaced itself, although the sun had set and no color lingered in the sky. It was a new moon at midsummer this year, so the effects were all the more startling.

"Nothing can make the summer solstice sinister," Molly said, though the whiteness of the sky did seem ghostly. Night blooming flowers shone bright on the dark ground, and the garden's starry beds sloped down to a silver stream. They walked to the water and looked across it at the black fields that rose above the farther bank. "Wolfi," Molly said. He'd been withdrawn all day, even before Healey had shocked them both into prolonged silence. "You have seen the films of Zborodny?"

"Yes."

"And you did not see your father there, did you?"

"No. But the point of the films, you recall, was to emphasize the zeal of the Ukrainians. The Germans were shadowy figures."

"Every village in Galicia has shrines by the roadside. We saw dozens of them as we drove."

"That is common sense."

"Then be sensible." His sorrow brought her close to tears. "Please, Wolfi. Don't torment yourself."

They walked a little longer, then returned to the cloisters and wished each other good night.

＊　＊　＊

SOME TIME later, Wolfi tapped lightly on her door and she opened it and let him in. "Close your curtain," he said. She'd left the window open for the beauty of the night and the smell of the new-mown hay. "And don't turn on a light. I want no one to know you're awake." She hurriedly did as he asked.

"Father Paul is not a Pole," he announced.

"What? How do you know?" The heavy curtains shut out all the light and as her eyes became adjusted to the darkness, she saw that Wolfi, who was wearing what he'd worn at dinner, carried a thick book and a flashlight.

"It kept ringing false, when Healey was expounding the priest's appalling views, but I was thinking of other things."

"Do you want a drink? I bought a bottle of that bison grass vodka."

"Please."

"I don't have a glass," she said. "Take a swig."

He took an inspiriting gulp and opened his Polish grammar book. " '*Ignatiku*,' " he began professorially, "is not a Polish form of Ignatius. In Polish, it's *Ignacy* and it is a rare name that does not change in the vocative, which is also *Ignacy*."

"Healey said it was a diminutive. Aren't there a dozen forms of every Slavic name, like Alexander and Alyushko and Alushchik and all the others that make it impossible to remember the characters in Russian novels?"

"The diminutive is *Ignas*." He showed her the table of diminutives. "And in the vocative, *Ignasie*."

"And didn't he also repeat a name Paul's mother used for him?"

"Yes," he said. "The Polish is *Pawlu* or *Pawelku* in the familiar form. He said something different, like *Pavlus*."

"So you think the words Healey remembers, that he prides himself on remembering verbatim, are Ukrainian?"

"This book"— Wolfi shone his flashlight now on its final pages—"is very complete. It's published in Stuttgart. The appendix compares Polish words with cognates in other Slavic languages and gives fifty of the most common given names."

"*Ignatiku*," she read, "and *Pavlus*. And remember the brandy with lemon and sugar? Have you seen that anywhere but in Ukraine?"

"No. The man is Ukrainian." Wolfi closed the grammar book.

"There can have been no reason for him to lie," Molly said emphatically, "apart from his role in the massacre. Emigré priests were welcomed in America. In most Catholic communities they were lionized, and any 'captive nation' was as good as another. They all looked alike." She had some of the bison grass vodka and handed the bottle to Wolfi.

"I must talk to Healey." Wolfi seemed prepared to do that immediately.

"Confront him, now?"

"Warn him. He has told the truth about Paul to a number of people who understood what he was saying."

"It's very late," she said. "And I don't think you should meet with him alone. You and I can talk with him first thing in the morning."

CHAPTER

$$\boxed{22}$$

Molly lay awake after Wolfi left: the irony of the affair now surpassed its horror. Ignatius Healey, she believed, had killed Caleb Tuttle to protect his mentor and tonight he himself had betrayed him: he'd revealed, to a gathering of scholars, clerics, and politically engaged intellectuals, that Father Paul was falsifying his past in a way that all but established his guilt.

She wished she were someplace where telephones worked, where a long-distance call did not require a half day's negotiation. She wanted to talk to Nick. More than to see him, or to feel his warmth and solidity and strength, she wanted to know what he thought. She loved him and, apart from that, she'd come to depend on his judgment. She didn't defer to him, but his sense of justice and sense of humor—of the fitness or absurdity of things—had become pole stars for her and she longed for him now.

She lit the candle by her bed. Usually she travelled with a serious book and an escapist book. Neither suited her tonight. She blew out the candle and opened the curtains. This short moonless night would be, for a few hours more, lit by starlight only. She heard popping noises, in rapid

166

succession, nor loud, but perhaps not near, and then a cry. She saw nothing moving in the gardens or in the fields beyond.

Her robe had fallen off the foot of her bed. She felt for it in the dark, found it, and put it on, and went out into the corridor. The stone floor was cool beneath her bare feet and she thought she was shivering because she was cold. Wolfi's room was three doors down from her own, along the same corridor. She knocked on the door. No answer. She knocked again.

Molly was exceedingly reluctant to force her way into Wolfi's bedroom: this was no time for false modesty, but neither was it time to panic. Possibly midsummer's night was celebrated in this part of the world with fireworks. The popping sounds she'd heard might not have been gunshots. They might have been Roman candles brought back from a visit to cousins in Buffalo—and the cry, an exclamation of delight as the sparklers were lit. The cry had not sounded like an exclamation of delight. She tried the door, which did not budge. It was locked and well fitted but opened, surprisingly easily, when she returned with a credit card and her own flashlight.

The room was empty; white cotton pajamas were folded at the foot of a bed that had not been slept in. The curtain was drawn and she shone her light around the room and under the bed. There she found a long case, a gun case, empty also. She'd been surprised when Wolfi inquired so closely about hunting. He was an outdoorsman of sorts, a rock-climber; but she didn't think he killed for sport. She looked briefly again around the bare, neat room. The Polish grammar book, a copy of the Vulgate, and a paperback edition of Nelly Sachs were stacked beside the bed. Molly could not read Nelly Sachs's poems about the Holocaust. She'd wakened screaming the one time, some years before, she'd tried to read them; she marvelled and grieved at the ordeals Wolfi put himself through.

And what was he putting himself through at this moment? He'd left no indication where he'd gone. Possibly he'd decided his talk with Healey could not wait till morning; perhaps he'd gone alone simply to spare her the unpleasantness. But why would he arm himself with a long-barrelled hunting rifle for this mission? Molly decided to get dressed and find out.

She went back to her room and put on a blouse, a light pullover sweater and a long full linen skirt with deep pockets that held her knife, flashlight, and handkerchief.

Molly had no notion where Ignatius Healey was spending the night. Most of the visiting scholars were staying in the cloisters, but she suspected Healey might have arranged more lavish quarters in the palace itself. She'd seen nothing of Healey in the cloisters and she thought she did not flatter herself in assuming he'd have paid her a visit if his room had been close to hers. Accordingly, she made her way along the rush-lit halls—the corridor lighting had been electrified but the fixtures looked like burning rushes—to the chapel, through which the cloisters were connected with the Elector's residence. The door that opened into the chapel swung noiselessly on well-oiled hinges: church buildings were well-maintained in Poland, and Molly slipped cautiously into the chapel. A light burned above the tabernacle and a blaze of candles illuminated a copy of the Madonna of Czestochowa before whom Adam Smith's young proselyte knelt in prayer.

Molly crossed to the door that led to the Palace and, finding it bolted and locked, returned to her room. She heard more popping noises, echoing in the night, and on an impulse snatched up the vodka and Bogdan's field glasses—he'd left them with her, saying he wouldn't need them in the city. She left the cloisters through a door that led to the garden paths and followed them to the terrace, which was muddy, as it had not been earlier. A person in muddy boots had crossed and recrossed the terrace, a person who'd come from the mown fields leaving bits of chaff and crushed wildflowers stuck in his muddy prints. Molly turned to look at the hayfields; the stream at the foot of the garden that had been so silvery before the light faded was now almost invisible, an inkier black than the sky.

She scanned the fields with Bogdan's binoculars. The night was dark, but she could make out, on one of the haystacks, an ungainly burden, as if a scarecrow had tried to climb the pole and become entangled in its cruel spikes. The figure was human, not some midsummer's effigy, and surely dead. This was not a scarecrow, clothing stuffed with straw, but a naked body hanging motionless on a hayrack in the middle of a shorn field. The starlight shone faintly on its whitish hair, tow-colored like the drying grass. Wolfi, Molly thought, no, anyone else, not you.

Molly might have been wiser to raise an alarm, but the body was so obviously dead. There was only blackness where its face had been, the face shot away. The hope that it was not, in fact, Wolfi—Poland was full of blond men and he was the only one whose death would devastate her—sped her on her way. She ran through the garden and tried to cross the stream on rocks spaced at awkward intervals. She fell, close to the opposite bank, and scrambled out of the water, dripping wet and bleeding from a scrape on her arm. Her flashlight still worked and the vodka bottle was unbroken. No harm done, but the haystack was farther than it appeared from the terrace. She found it difficult to judge distances at night and the undulations of the hayfield had been invisible from the terrace, whose elevation she'd also misjudged. She'd seen in daylight that the gardens sloped away from the palace and the fields rose on the other side of the stream, but she hadn't grasped the difficulty of the terrain. She thought that if she kept going uphill she'd find the right haystack. It had been set on a prominent rise.

She plunged on and, suddenly, the body was looming over her, faceless, with vicious spikes through its chest and abdomen. Resolutely, she took out her flashlight. She thought she'd try the hands first, and she fell to her knees on the sharp stubble when she saw the short, pink, pudgy fingers of Ignatius Healey. Wolfi's hands were small also but brown and scarred from rock-climbing.

She knelt, trembling with relief, not certain she could stand, and listened to the night. She heard nothing, no wind, just cricketlike noises in the stubble and some night birds calling, harsh and unmelodic. Her long skirt was wet around her legs, chilling her; she began, slowly recovering from an agony of terror, to think about her position. She shone her light on the torso: the chest and abdomen were bloody; he'd been alive when those wounds were inflicted. Healey had been impaled and then shot. His body was meant to be found—rough justice arising, no doubt, out of last evening's lapse—and the mowers would be in the fields at first light; but was anyone lurking, watching, making sure the body remained undisturbed until then?

Molly had heard two series of shots, separated by perhaps twenty minutes. She was concluding she would do well to leave the hayfield when a voice called feebly to her, and she ran to find Wolfi, who lay at the base of another haystack, resting his head against the sweet-smelling grass. His shirt was soaked with blood. He'd been shot in the shoulder or upper arm, and a bullet had grazed his temple, leaving a red welt that oozed blood.

"How are you?" she asked.

"Not so bad." She saw he'd bitten through his lips to keep from crying out. "What are you doing here?"

"You called me."

"I did not," he roused himself to protest.

"I thought you did."

"You saw poor Healey?"

"Yes."

"*Kein Delikatesse,*" he said and fainted.

She wet her handkerchief with bison vodka and wiped his face. She hoped it might act in some measure as smelling salts and he stirred in response to it. "Wolfi," she said. "I know nothing about bullet wounds. What should I do?"

"You should leave."

"That I will not do." She took her knife from the pocket of her skirt. "Let me cut away your shirt," she said. "Are you shot anyplace else?" She remembered reading of gunshot victims who'd died in emergency rooms because some exhausted resident had treated one wound and neglected to examine the patient for any other.

"Not that I can feel," he said.

The small sharp scissors on her knife cut cleanly through the fine broadcloth. "It doesn't look too bad, Wolfi. Blood's not spurting." No artery appeared to be damaged, but she was worried about shock. He was shaking and he seemed to be losing interest in her actions. "Was Healey brought here naked?" she asked, hoping to cover him with Healey's clothes, if she could find them. Her linen skirt, even were it dry, would provide little warmth.

"He had a raincoat over his pajamas," Wolfi said. "I saw them take him from his room."

Maybe they, whoever they were, had left his clothes. They'd done nothing else to disguise their crime. After a few minutes, Molly located a pair of Liberty of London silk paisley pajamas and a wool-lined Burberry raincoat.

She cut the silk into pieces, doused them with vodka and made a rough bandage. Then she covered Wolfi with Healey's raincoat.

The sky was brightening in the east and Healey's body was meant to be found. Would the people who staged that exemplary vengeance come back to make sure their message wasn't lost on whoever did find it?

"Can you walk?" she asked.

"You can go now. Day's breaking. People will soon be coming."

She shook her head; he reached out to her, to touch her while he reasoned with her, and felt that her sleeve was wet. "You came across the brook?" he said. "Directly up from the garden? Molly, please, you must not stay."

"Where's your gun? Do you know?" She'd been debating for some time whether to ask this question.

"I dropped it," he said, "when I was hit. I was unconscious for a time afterward . . . Go, now, please."

"I'm going to look for a wagon." She would not leave Wolfi to be found by people who thought they'd already killed him. She protected him to a degree, she understood, by simply staying with him. She'd be a witness to whatever happened; three corpses, two of them American, would be a lot to explain. But that meant she could not leave him to get help.

And he needed more help than she could give. He'd lost a lot of blood and he ought to be treated as soon as possible. He'd been shot in the right chest, below the shoulder joint, but, she thought, clear of the lung. He wasn't coughing; if no vital organ was involved, she reasoned, moving him posed no additional danger, except possibly that movement might provoke more bleeding. She wasn't sure how to assess that risk, but it paled before the other dangers she feared.

Near an immense haystack, Molly found a flat bed wagon such as Bogdan had described, a narrow platform without sides, with poles for handles. She wheeled it over to Wolfi and tilted it, roughly parallel with his body, against the haystack. He resisted, but she pleaded and, at last, helped him to shift himself onto the wagon, from which she feared he'd any moment fall. The belt of Healey's Burberry, though generous, wasn't long enough to lash him in place; Molly took off her sweater and cut her blouse into strips—silk was strong, she knew, used at one time for parachutes—and twisted and tied it into a cord, which when added to Healey's belt sufficed to bind Wolfi to the wagon. The improvised rope did not hold him securely, but it helped.

Her plan was to move him diagonally across the sloping fields to the road she knew lay at the southern edge of the pasture. If she tried to take Wolfi directly down she'd lose control of the wagon as it gained momentum. Fortunately the handles were rough; they tore the skin of her palms, leaving deep splinters, but a smoother wood might have slipped altogether from her grasp. Even on a gentle incline, she found it hard to control the wagon's speed. She decided to turn it and pull rather than push, using all her weight to brake its progress.

The jolting did not seem to have reopened Wolfi's wound, and she felt confident she'd chosen right, or at least not chosen wrong. He was delirious now and spoke, brokenly, avowals painful for her to hear, finally calling, in deeper abandon, for his mother.

She'd gotten him almost to the road when Ivan Vorenchuk, the zealot from Sevastopol, came loping across the pasture, running faster when he sighted her. "I thought I saw lights over here last night. My God, what has happened? Have you been here with Ritter all night?"

"I heard noises that I thought might have been gunshots," she explained, " and when I went to look I found Wolfi."

"My dear young woman, how could you have been so

foolish as to go out alone, not knowing what dangers you were exposing yourself to?" He felt free to upbraid her and she resented the authority he assumed.

She had to admit he posed a fair question. Apart from Wolfi, she knew no one at the conference well. Wattle, she knew by reputation and felt to be dependable, and some of the Americans were decent men; but she did not think any of them would have rushed out into the night with her on the basis of the story she'd have told them. She'd looked to nobody but Wolfi for practical help and he'd been missing.

"I thought no one would take me seriously," she said. "And then I saw a body I knew to be dead."

"You thought to be dead," he corrected her. "You will be all right, Ritter." Vorenchuk had been examining Wolfi, gently and competently as he spoke. "I spent ten years as a hospital orderly on account of my unsound political views before I was permitted to enter university."

"I can't say I'm sorry," Ritter said, weakly. He lapsed in and out of consciousness.

Molly looked questioningly at Vorenchuk.

"I am as certain as a man can be who is not a physician himself. You're fond of him?" She supposed he might excuse her rash behavior on those grounds.

"He's my friend."

"And it is well you went to him. I would have found him eventually, but you have comforted him and kept him warm."

"There is another body," she said. "And it's definitely beyond our help."

"Then," Vorenchuk said, taking the poles of the wagon in his strong hands, "let us save whom we can." He maneuvered the wagon onto the road. "Run along beside and see he doesn't slip off. Tell me if I'm going too fast." He pulled the wagon at a steady trot that was not easy for Molly to match. They ran along the dirt road, Vorenchuk managing to steer around the deepest ruts, until the Elector's palace appeared before them. "Who's the other," he asked. "Healey?"

"Yes."

"The fool," Vorenchuk said. "I tried myself to warn him."

CHAPTER

23

IGNATIUS HEALEY was not so famous as he might have fancied himself and, horrific as the circumstances of his death had been, they'd yielded no film footage. Then too, he'd been primarily a print journalist, so the electronic media paid little attention to his passing.

Homicide always got a little crazy towards the end of June, not with violent deaths but with weddings, graduations, and family trips that had to be fitted in between the end of school and the beginning of summer camp. Officers with families took their vacations and Nick Hannibal happily filled in for them, looking forward to those cloudless summers to come when younger cops would do the same for him. He hadn't seen a paper for some time.

Nick spent the day in court waiting to testify in the case of a man who'd shot his former girlfriend, their two children, and her new boyfriend on Patriots' Day as they boarded a swanboat in the Public Gardens. The defendant, who gave his name as Paul Revere, said he'd fired only to warn them of the approaching redcoats; his lawyer wanted to bar jurors skeptical of reincarnation. Little had been accomplished by four o'clock, when court recessed and Nick headed for Fenway Park.

The Sox, back from the road, were playing the A's at home in a twinight doubleheader; Nick thought he'd catch the first game before he went back to work. Roger Clemens was hot; he had a no-hitter going into the eighth and Jose Canseco was striking out on a slider that sank about two feet when Nick's beeper sounded. For an instant, he thought of drowning it, dropping the bleeping nuisance into his waxed cup of warm beer, but discipline held. He swore softly and made his way, past fans who swore loudly, to the aisle and out to the phones.

He dialed a number he did not recognize and John, Cardinal Hollihan, answered.

"No, Your Eminence, you didn't take me away from anything important. The noise? Nothing, Your Eminence, just a ballgame." The crowd was howling: at a bad call? a walk? an error? It wasn't a jubilant sound, more like a collective shriek of rage: an error scored as a hit? the irredeemably bleeping shortstop? "I'm sorry, I didn't hear you. Shot and then what? Impaled, Your Eminence, but not in cruciform position? *Near Krakow?*" Yes, Nick found it shocking. More than shocking.

The cardinal told him that he'd met with Ignatius Healey, God rest his soul, before the man left the country and he'd been troubled by some things he'd said about Caleb Tuttle. Perhaps he ought to have gotten in touch with the Boston police sooner, but he'd feared his—Nick was sure the cardinal stopped himself from saying "suspicions"—his misgivings were farfetched. Would Nick come to Pennsylvania to talk with him? His doctors were mother hens and they wanted him to rest.

"Your Eminence," Nick said. "I'm on my way. I'll call you from the airport and let you know when to expect me."

"Jeez," the cabbie said, turning down his radio, as Nick told him to get to Logan as fast as he could. "You must be in some kinda hurry, if you're willing to leave this game. I never heard of nothing like what happened in the top of the eighth."

When they got to the airport Nick leapt out of the cab. He had not heard a word the man said. "Wait here. I may need to go to another terminal." US Air had a flight to Philadelphia in forty-five minutes, he learned, and no other airline had one sooner. He paid his cab fare, bought a ticket, and called Homicide.

Capt. Riordan told him he'd given the cardinal his beeper number. Cardinal Hollihan had called the Commissioner for the name of the officer in charge of the Tuttle case; later the cardinal had called him, the senior captain in homocide, and asked how to get in touch with Nick. The cardinal had spoken, so far as Riordan knew, to no one else in the department and he'd emphasized that his interest in the matter was unofficial and must be kept absolutely confidential.

"I'm going to see him," Nick said. "He may want me to go to Poland."

"Sure he will." Riordan laughed. "How long's Molly been gone? See what the cardinal has to say about Tuttle and come right back. Paul Revere's got to get to ev'ry Middlesex village and farm. I don't want us to hold him up."

Nick had some time before boarding and checked his messages at home. His mother was worried about Molly; an American writer had been killed in Poland. Molly's mother had called too, less apprehensive, but more aware of her daughter's opinion of Healey. *Had* he, as it happened, Mary Rafferty asked, talked with Molly recently and would he call her back? He hadn't, but Molly told him when she left Vienna that she probably wouldn't try to call again. East of Vienna, long-distance calls were hard to arrange.

The last message was left in the savvy, gravelly voice of the man from the Anti-Defamation League. Nick had liked him when they'd talked earlier and given him his home number. "This script, Lieutenant. We've never seen it. Most of the anecdotes come from *Mittel-europa*, such a hellhole, but filmwise it mixes up the angry villagers from *Frankenstein* with the rape in *Birth of a Nation*. That one never fails. Look at Willy Horton. Sorry we can't be more help."

CARDINAL HOLLIHAN sent his assistant Timothy Lynch to the Philadelphia airport to meet the detective who'd obligingly caught a late flight from Boston. Father Lynch, newly ordained, was punctual; he always allowed plenty of time. On the return trip, he continued to drive carefully, obeying the speed limit and pointing out local sights. He was unable to tell his passenger anything about Ignatius Healey's death that the cardinal had not already told him.

When they got to King of Prussia, Nick Hannibal asked how the town's name had escaped being changed during the First World War. Father Lynch had no idea; he'd grown up outside of Philadelphia and the question had never occurred to him. Nick Hannibal told him peremptorily to stop and he slammed on the brakes.

"I'm sorry," Nick apologized, embarrassed. "I'm preoccupied about something. Would you mind if I drove?"

THE CARDINAL, though under the strictest instructions to rest, waited for them on his porch swing, watching stars twinkle through the honeysuckle vines. The children were sleeping in the big barn he'd had converted into dormitories; lights-out had been hours before, but from time to time he heard whispering and suppressed giggles. He loved to listen to them.

Nicholas Hannibal sounded like an interesting man. After he'd gotten Nick's name from the Commissioner, Hollihan had called the police department's personnel office where, he correctly anticipated, the clerk would be a good Irish or Italian girl, willing to look up some information for him. He'd emphasized that he didn't want medical or disciplinary records, nothing that should properly be kept confidential. Could she find out for him where a Lt. Hannibal had gone to high school? How old he was? Was he married and, if he wasn't married, who should be notified in an emergency? "Oh, he's getting married," she answered and the cardinal heard a twinge of regret in her voice. She'd found the other information quickly and he thanked her for it.

Thirty-three and he'd gone to B.C. High? That made it easy. There'd be priests around still who'd taught him; and the cardinal wanted a little background on Hannibal. It wasn't as easy as he'd hoped: he'd called the principal's office and asked how many of the faculty had been teaching between fifteen and twenty years. Not too many, and the head of the math department who'd taught calculus for twenty-five years was in Rome for the summer. There'd been a lot of turnover in history and science: men had left teaching and others had left the Church. Continuity, the principal's assistant thought, was to be found in classical languages, and he gave the cardinal some names. Was there any particular aspect of the school His Eminence wished to know about?

The cardinal answered with a mental reservation and tried a man who taught Cicero. He remembered Nick Hannibal well: A quick learner who did not coast by, as he easily could have, on his marked ability. With a temper he got a bit better at controlling before he graduated. Liked Roman history and the republican writers. Read some Livy and was caught reading Machiavelli's *Discourses* on Livy when the religion faculty thought him too young to resist so seductive a paganism. The Machiavelli incident was the most serious trouble he got into in high school. Girls? He'd been a decent boy and intelligent enough to be discreet.

His family? That was a story. His father had been shot when Nick was about thirteen in a drive-by shooting. Apparently completely fortuitous. Immigrant father, name had been Annibale, with no mob ties. The boy's mother was a formidable woman. When the people responsible for the shooting tried to make it right, she'd refused their money. Repeatedly refused. He was an only son and his mother doted on him. The old Latinist hadn't heard about the impending marriage. Hannibal was the type who got on with his life; he didn't come to reunions.

CARDINAL HOLLIHAN took these pains to learn a few things about Nick Hannibal because he was thinking of confiding in him a matter of grave concern. He hadn't liked Ignatius Healey, but that was beside the point. He had contempt for Healey's kind of Catholic, incense-choked bigots who thought history was all downhill since the Inquisition. They were bad and dangerous and wrong, but this was worse. He hoped that Healey hadn't killed Tuttle and that, if he had, he hadn't died unrepentant. This was far worse: an urgent call from Krakow—the Polish bishops had a great phone system, legacy of the Solidarity days—brought news far more alarming than word of Healey's death.

"Your Eminence," Timothy Lynch reproached him. "You should be in bed."

John, Cardinal Hollihan, rose from the swing and extended his hand in a manner that enabled a visitor, without discourtesy, to kiss his ring or not to kiss it. Nick Hannibal chose to shake his hand, the custom the cardinal himself preferred.

"Would you rather talk in the morning, Lieutenant?" he asked.

Nick was burning to find out everything the cardinal knew, but he was faced with a man who was plainly not well. "Whichever you prefer, Your Eminence. I'm not tired."

The cardinal thought Hannibal looked haggard, but he himself was impatient. "Perhaps for a few minutes? Timmy, you go to bed."

Lynch looked worse than Hannibal: the drive from Philadelphia had harrowed his soul and he wanted to give thanks for his survival. He said good-night and urged that the cardinal not tax his strength.

"Were any other Americans involved . . . hurt . . . along with Healey?" Nick had been unable to put this question to a voice that belonged to a man he'd never met. He wanted to be looking into the speaker's eyes when he heard the answer.

"No, none, not at all or only peripherally. He was attending some sort of academic affair. I didn't mean to order you down here, as if it were the crime of the century," the cardinal said.

"I came because I think you can help." Nick was able now to give the cardinal his full attention. He appeared to be the man he was loved and ridiculed for being, direct and unpretentious. He wore a plaid woolen bathrobe over striped pajamas and motioned for Nick to join him on a porch swing with cushions neatly mended and faded from years of summer sun.

Nick didn't follow church politics closely, but it had

struck him on the flight that several other American cardinals, who aspired to a greater role in public life, would be more concerned with Ignatius Healey's life and death than Hollihan was likely to be. Any of them would have an excellent avenue through which to investigate a murder in Poland. John, Cardinal Hollihan, had wanted to talk about Tuttle's death, not Healey's.

"You know about this priest the Ukrainians want to try for war crimes? Yes? I guess the world knows. It rattles some ugly skeletons."

"And it's your decision?"

"In large part. If I order him to give himself up, we, this country, will extradite him."

Nick thought cover-ups, even well executed, put the institutions that attempted them at risk, and nothing did as much harm as a botched cover-up. The cardinal hadn't asked his advice, but that's what he thought.

The cardinal was thinking along the same lines. "We gain nothing, the Church, by stonewalling. Politics is played in the real world. It's flawed, no political player's untainted . . . "

Nick here substituted the word "infallible." The cardinal avoided technical terms.

"I admit my mistakes," Hollihan concluded. "I've made my share."

"I'm glad it's your call, sir." Nick had, unconsciously, begun to regard him as a chief rather than a prelate.

"Not yours, you mean?" He pushed his feet further into his slippers, setting the swing in motion.

"Not any of the other American cardinals."

"You're not a regular churchgoer?"

"No."

"Healey came to me before he left the country," Hollihan said, seemingly undismayed by Nick's admission. "He begged me to put off my decision until he got back. I frankly thought he meant to find or manufacture another suspect, and that Tuttle's death left him a freer hand to do that."

"What made you think ... " This was some hunch even for a man who knew a lot about evil.

"He seemed desperately uneasy. He fed me gossip about the gardener's boy and the housekeeper's nephew. He wanted Tuttle's murder to be squalid and domestic, but above all, over and done. And he seemed frightened. I believe he genuinely loved Father Paul."

Nick put forth the facts as he saw them: that Healey had almost certainly been present at the meal during which Tuttle had been poisoned; and that, though he need not have administered the poison himself, he had escaped its effects in ways that raised hard questions. Healey had attempted to contact the great-nephew, Charlie Smith, who'd received other mysterious long-distance calls and whose connection with the poisoning had been established fairly well, if not yet beyond a reasonable doubt. The broken vinegar bottle had yielded no fingerprints.

"But what do you hear from Poland?" he asked the cardinal.

"Healey's body, as I told you on the phone, was savaged in an old-fashioned way. The local authorities believe historians and anthropologists know more about the custom than the farmers do."

"Healey was at this academic affair."

"You put two and two together quickly, my boy."

"My fiancée's there too, and she's an historian."

The cardinal had wondered why he'd asked about other Americans. "My goodness, is she? The world's changing, isn't it? Policemen's wives and sweethearts always did a lot of worrying. I suspect worrying's harder on men."

"But men may look forward to vengeance," Nick said.

"Caleb Tuttle tracked down the men who murdered the woman he loved." That seemed relevant somehow.

"During the war? When killing's a duty? I killed a man myself, one that I know about, with my bayonet, just outside of Cherbourg."

"After my father died," Nick remembered—he'd never told Molly this. He'd been so ashamed when it happened he'd repressed the memory and not thought of it until this moment—"I wanted to kill the man I thought was responsible."

The Latin teacher had been informative, the cardinal thought, but I bet he hadn't known about this. "You were, how old?"

"Thirteen, almost fourteen. My mother found my knife and threw it away." He said this dazedly as though he'd just realized his knife was missing.

"You'll be a better father yourself for your love of him," Cardinal Hollihan said, going into his study to give Nick a moment to recover. He returned with two kitchen tumblers of Irish whiskey. Some ladies' group had given him Waterford crystal but he never used it.

"What really worries me about Healey's death," the cardinal said, after they'd finished the first round and he'd sent Nick for the bottle to pour a second, "is that suspicion's cast on a fine man, a very good man, who may not live to defend himself. A German called Wolfgang Ritter."

"I've got to talk to Molly, sir. She's fond of Ritter."

CHAPTER

$$\boxed{24}$$

Molly maintained her composure until they got to the hospital. She and Ivan Vorenchuk spoke with the director of the conference center and decided that sending for an ambulance would take too long. The center owned an old panel truck; they'd put a mattress in the back and take Ritter to Krakow themselves. The director sent for the handyman who usually drove the truck and went to see about a mattress.

While they waited in the palace's pebbled driveway for the director's return, a man Molly knew slightly—a careful fellow from Princeton who worked on John Knox—came out to jog and she asked him to get Gervase Wattle. She hoped Wattle would come with them: he was resourceful and he might be able to locate Bogdan Soltan, who, she thought, would be helpful in dealing with whatever bureaucratic problems they faced. The hospital, she'd been informed, was midway between Krakow and Nowa Huta, serving both the old and the new cities.

There were other clinics in Krakow, closer to the medical school; but Ivan Vorenchuk argued, and the center's director concurred, that the central hospital, which dealt with industrial accidents was best prepared for this kind of trauma and, accordingly, the place to take Ritter. Molly thought that made sense and she explained their reasoning to Gervase Wattle, who'd come on the run, unshaven and wearing unmatched socks, like the brick he was.

"My Lord," he said, seeing the pallet on which Ritter was still lying. "You just trussed him up and wheeled him in? Good show, my dear. Didn't know he wore a Burberry."

Ritter was unconscious, but Wattle, who'd been sixteen when the war ended, had drunk in his father's and uncles' and brothers' war stories and absorbed a certain amount of battlefield lore. He grasped both of Ritter's hands firmly and assured him that he'd soon be up and about in absolutely tip-top form. He was feeling rotten at the moment possibly, but they'd have him patched up in no time, good as new.

Ritter opened his eyes and closed them again. He must have expected to see Lord Mountbatten or the Queen Mum, Molly thought.

Wolfi had responded, nonetheless, to Wattle's cheerfulness; he heard what was being said around him, and she nerved herself to be no less brisk and encouraging. "We thought he'd be more comfortable lying down. Ivan Vorenchuk actually got him here." Then she explained that the raincoat belonged to Ignatius Healey and that Healey was dead.

Wattle made a peculiar noise, a choking harrumph, an arrested snort. "Can't say I'm surprised. I suppose we ought to notify the police. What have the Poles got for police these days? Still under the Ministry of Interior? Bad lot, they used to be. Gendarmerie? Some sort of regional or departmental forces? Don't worry, my dear, the local people will know whom to call. Our job's getting Wolfi patched up."

That job proved more difficult than Molly could have imagined. Wattle had come along, sitting in front with the driver; she and Vorenchuk rode in back with Wolfi. The director followed in his own car. The phones were not working at the palace that morning and he'd notify the police about Ignatius Healey after completing the requisite forms at the hospital. Gunshot wounds, he explained, were not common in Poland and, therefore, as with any unusual circumstance, necessitated the filing of a series of extremely detailed forms.

The hospital had quantities of blank forms. It did not have whole blood, surgical gloves, or any intravenous antibiotics. "I regret profoundly the lack of blood," the chief of surgery apologized. He'd trained in Paris and understood how appalled foreigners must be by these shortages. "We lost electricity for three days last week and the auxiliary generator did not suffice to maintain refrigeration. A most unhappy circumstance about which, I assure you, I do not know how to express my regret."

"Can't you use plasma?" Vorenchuk was prepared to cope but Molly was not.

She was sobbing with rage and grief. "We've got to get him out of here," she said to Wattle. "We've got to get him to a country where things work. What's it like in Prague?"

"Prague is better, madame," the doctor said. "But, madame, I am desolated, he cannot be moved."

Molly wept, helplessly.

"Stabilize him." Wattle handed Molly a clean handkerchief as he gave this instruction. Her own was stiff with dried blood and smelled strongly of vodka. "And we'll take him to Germany. British consulate's on the Rynek, Germans must be nearby. I'll see what I can do. About an hour's flying time to Frankfurt, isn't it? Berlin's even closer." And he ran off, prepared to commandeer a plane.

Vorenchuk stood by her as Wolfi was wheeled into another room. "They will use plasma," he said. "Whole blood isn't necessary. It's blood volume that's critical. And they will need to irrigate the wound and probe it for bullet fragments. They can use distilled water to do that. Antibiotics aren't needed at this stage."

"I suppose they've got anesthesia?" Vorenchuk's mastery of the situation had calmed her.

"He won't feel much," Vorenchuk said. "There's a lassitude that comes . . ."

"It's very bad, isn't it?" Molly felt that she would not break down again and wanted an honest prognosis. Wolfi had seemed to be ebbing away.

"The wound should not be fatal."

"But?"

"Your instinct is correct. You and Ritter are not lovers, are you?"

"No."

"I thought not," this profoundly traditional man observed, "but you must not blame yourself."

THE DIRECTOR returned with an inspector from the regional constabulary, who told them that a representative of the investigational division of the Ministry of the Interior would be arriving shortly. The inspector rehearsed for them, with the director and Vorenchuk translating, his initial impressions of the past night's events. Two persons had been shot, Professor Ritter, who was being treated here, and an American journalist, now deceased, whose body had not yet been removed from the pole to which it was affixed due to a shortage of film for the cameras of the constabulary's photographic division. Film had been stolen from their storeroom and devoted, they'd recently discovered, to the production of a clandestine pornographic magazine, which had enjoyed great success locally and was now available in Western Europe as well. Fortunately, no, fortunately was not exactly what the man meant, but it happened to his advantage that because the deceased was an American, he'd been able to enlist the aid of the American consulate, which had sent a photographer to the scene. Shortly they hoped to remove the body to the police morgue and commence an autopsy.

Peasants had discovered Ignatius Healey's body at first light, exhibited as it was so conspicuously on a small hill. The country folk had sent a boy on a bicycle to summon a village policeman, who had returned with him and driven back the considerable throng, including many distinguished professors from abroad, who had gathered in the hayfield to view the naked corpse. The local officer had been able to do little more than keep the crowd at bay, but when the crime was reported to the proper authorities—as the director ought immediately to have done although one understood his concern to attend first to the injured—an adequate police force was dispatched, albeit regrettably with insufficient film for their cameras.

Be that as it may, squadrons were sent in sufficient numbers to undertake a systematic investigation of the surrounding fields and of the palace, with particular attention to the rooms of Professor Ritter and the deceased Mr. Healey. Both these shootings had occurred close to the Elector's summer palace, where a conference was being conducted; both men had attended the opening session of the conference the previous evening. It seemed likely that they knew each other and also that they together knew a number of third parties. This morning, police would begin interviewing the participants in the conference. He expected a preliminary report before the end of the day.

His recital occupied perhaps twenty minutes, allowing

for translation, and diverted Molly to some extent from her complicated worries about Wolfi. She'd been so intent on his plight that she'd scarcely thought about Healey. She assumed the killer or killers—could one man have hoisted Healey on that haypole? possibly, she thought, but not likely, or perhaps the body could have been skewered on the ground and then levered into position—the killers, she inclined to the plural, had in any event, thankfully, been too intent on their grisly task to search out Wolfi where he'd fallen.

The two unfortunate victims, the inspector continued, might together or independently, have ventured into the fields beyond the palace gardens, and there encountered ruffians. Robbery could have been a motive and such amounts of money and traveller's checks that might be found in their rooms would be compared with the amounts set forth in their currency declarations.

Molly could not imagine why this tale was being told at such length in the waiting room of a hospital.

"I cannot, however, exclude the possibility"—Ivan Vorenchuk blanched as he translated this sentence—"the possibility that the two men shot each other."

"Ask him," Molly said, "whether he thinks Healey shot Wolfi after Wolfi impaled him on the haypole or whether Wolfi managed to do that without using his right arm."

"He says he does not know precisely the manner in which the crimes were accomplished," Vorenchuk said. "But he wants to hold everyone's passport."

The surgeon came at that moment, wiping blood from his ungloved hands, to tell them that the patient was no weaker. He had not attempted any aggressive intervention, merely cleaned the wound as best he could and sedated the patient as heavily as he thought prudent. "Possibly, madame," he said, "your husband might be flown to Germany later in the day. I would wish to monitor his vital signs for a few hours before attempting to move him."

"Pan Ritter is our colleague," Ivan Vorenchuk explained. "Not this lady's husband. We are all deeply concerned about him."

"Naturally. Forgive me, madame."

"It was a natural mistake, " Molly said. "And we are all grateful for the care you've given him."

The inspector spoke to the doctor in Polish and then cut short his reply. They exchanged angry words for some minutes until they were interrupted by the German consul, who'd come in with Wattle, unnoticed as the argument grew more heated.

"What on earth do you mean Herr Ritter cannot return to Germany for treatment?" The consul spoke Polish well but asked his question in English. He wanted to alert Wattle to the problem and to shift the debate to a language he expected he spoke better than most Polish policemen.

"He is suspected of a crime."

"He is the victim of a crime," the consul countered. "There is," he addressed the surgeon, "a regularly scheduled Lufthansa flight to Berlin at two this afternoon and another to Frankfurt at four-fifteen. Which would you advise?"

The doctor preferred the later flight: it allowed more time to establish that the patient was strong enough to make the trip.

"What's his blood type?" the diplomat asked. "The pilot will radio ahead. Oh, you did not? Never mind, we can get it from his army records. They're computerized. I'll have a vehicle at your disposal at three o'clock. Would you be good enough to accompany Ritter to the airport yourself? There will be two doctors on the Frankfurt flight. We've checked the passenger manifest."

"This man will not leave Poland," the inspector announced, "without clearance from the Ministry of Justice and from the Foreign Cooperation Office of the Ministry of the Interior. I do not have the authority to permit his exit pending communication from Warsaw. Possibly also the assent of the Foreign Minister must be secured."

"Are you going to stand about waiting for orders from your superiors when life is at stake?" The earnest, efficient German consul was fully thirty years younger than the Polish policeman across whose face an indescribable expression was passing.

Molly shared some of the feelings the policeman would not attempt to put into words, and she hastened to try another approach. "You want Ritter alive to stand trial, don't you?"

"I cannot take responsibility."

"I'll be back at three o'clock," the consul said, leaving to explore other options. He wheeled around at the door and took a gold-edged leather notebook from his breast pocket, handing it with a tiny golden mechanical pencil to the doctor. "Make a list of everything you need to treat him, if it must be done here."

The surgeon scribbled a wish list of pharmaceuticals and the consul faxed it to Frankfurt as soon as he got back to his office.

It was fortunate he did that because when he returned to the hospital, the Polish police were more adamant than they'd previously been and an official from the Ministry of the Interior implacable: Ritter's gun—or a rifle identical to one missing from a case under Ritter's bed—had been found in tall grass in the field from which Ignatius Healey's body had at last been removed. An old woman had struck it with her scythe and been frightened but unhurt when it discharged its last cartridge.

CHAPTER

25

"RITTER'S MISTRESS," Helmut Schluessel sneered, "what do you expect her to say?" He had offered his services to the authorities investigating the death of his friend, Ignatius Healey.

Molly was pointing out that Wolfgang Ritter had no reason to kill Healey hours after he had, in effect, conceded the guilt of a man Ritter was determined to bring to justice. Ritter was a good man but even if he were a bad man, Healey had become invaluable to him.

"An overeducated American woman who's had, no doubt, any number of Jewish lovers. What do you expect her to say when her paramour kills, possibly at her instigation, a man who dares to question lies that have too long passed for truth?"

"You ineffable cur." Gervase Wattle almost levitated in his fury.

They were gathered, Schluessel, Molly, Vorenchuk, Wattle, the regional inspector, and police officials from several other Polish agencies and bureaus, in a hospital staff meeting room. The police had taken statements from Molly and Vorenchuk, who acknowledged being in

194

the fields at dawn, and now permitted, even encouraged, them all to talk together.

"You are not worth the hemp for hanging," Wattle said, mastering his rage.

"Precisely," Schluessel exulted. "In just such terms did Ritter threaten me, publicly, last week in Vienna. If I had not left the conference last night to return to the hunting lodge where I have been staying with a large party of my compatriots, he might have slain me also."

"You do wrong to insult this lady, Schluessel. But you do well to remind the police," Ivan Vorenchuk noted, "that many foreigners come to shoot in Poland."

The gun, which Molly had not doubted was Wolfi's, had been identified by a Krakow gunsmith licensed under the Game and Wildlife Bureau of the Forestry Division of the Ministry of Tourism as a hunting rifle rented to Pan Ritter, who was duly furnished with a hunting license issued in Vienna and who had come to his shop the previous morning with another gentleman.

Polish practice, a lucrative one Molly gathered, was to insist that foreign sportsmen rent guns and buy ammunition from a small number of authorized dealers. In the fall, it was possible for a fee to arrange an import license for one's own firearms, but most of the year, guns were rented at a high daily rate. Vorenchuk raised an interesting possibility: that Schluessel had a similar, possibly an identical, gun. Wolfi had mentioned, when they'd arrived in Lviv, his suspicion that Schluessel was in the area and armed.

But Molly thought they should reveal none of their own ideas in Schluessel's presence. Wolfi had been right in telling Nick about the three kinds of Nazis. Schluessel, she believed to be intelligent and knew to be dishonest: she'd seen him vouching for forged documents. She wondered to what or to whom he might be loyal. Healey, she thought, had been loyal to a fault. Possibly he'd also been honest.

"Shall I describe what happened?" Schluessel told rather than asked the Polish interrogators. "Healey was lured into the garden, and thence into the fields, by Miss Rafferty."

"That's right," Molly said. "I always celebrate midsummer's night in hayfields with men in paisley silk pajamas. I order them specially from London."

"Molly, take care." Vorenchuk was dismayed, then realized that she was goading Schluessel, hoping he would say more.

"I believe poor Ignatius did not long remain clad in his English pajamas."

Molly believed that too: the pajamas had been clean when she'd cut them up for bandages. They were soaked now with Wolfi's blood, but Healey had not been shot while wearing them. She was interested to learn Schluessel seemed to know that.

"So you seduced him and whilst he was inflamed with passion, your accomplices set upon him . . ."

There must be blood on the ground, Molly was thinking, and not just at the foot of the pole. They must have stripped him and driven the spikes though him while he was lying on the ground. But the first cry came after the first shots, and it was just a cry. A man would be in prolonged agony while being skewered with those thorny branches. Wolfi said he saw Healey being carried off. And Healey was silent then too, or one of the several dozen people sleeping in the palace would have heard him. Healey took a bottle of brandy with him from the terrace. Did he also use sleeping pills? He complained about coping with jet lag and new time zones. If he'd been zonked— or chloroformed. Was chloroform used in Poland? Medicine was decades in arrears here, perhaps crime was also—if Healey had been unconscious, deeply unconscious, they could have staked him and killed him before Wolfi got there.

"And who potted Ritter?" Wattle asked.

"I believe you did," Schluessel said. He'd spent much of the morning at the palace. "I have learned that you were in the gardens as late as two in the morning."

"So I was," Wattle said, "with that young man who's so taken with Adam Smith. He was shaken by the dreadful things Healey'd been saying. I was telling him about Smith's notion of 'fellow-feeling,' natural sympathy and so on."

Wattle was introducing a Polish seminarian to *The Theory of Moral Sentiments*, Molly thought; a good night's work.

"He said he left you at two and went into the chapel to pray." Schluessel sounded confident. "I imagine he fled temptation."

Molly reckoned she had seen the boy kneeling before the madonna a little after two. She had not seen Wattle anywhere.

"It was a moonless night," the police inspector objected. "And Pan Ritter was not shot from close range. How is it that his friend could have shot him?"

"An old coward's trick," Schluessel replied. "It's nothing new. And Wattle may have done more damage than he intended."

Nothing new, Schluessel said. Molly wanted to beat him at this game. Overeducated for a woman, was she? Educated enough to know *Im Westen Nichts Neues* as the German title of *All Quiet on the Western Front*. And in that wrenching novel the story was told of German conscripts who shot themselves in the foot or lower leg so as to be invalided out of the trenches. When officers began executing soldiers with obviously self-inflicted wounds, the men shot one another at longer range. Sometimes, they shot badly and killed their comrade. Sometimes they missed. But their officers never knew whether a friend or an enemy sniper was responsible. Had it been Schluessel's plan to injure but not to kill Healey? To secure a lengthy convalescence during which he could not repeat, in court, the testimony he'd given about Paul's mother tongue? Schluessel's theory suggested a number of possibilities.

"Wattle shot him," Helmut Schluessel said, repeating his accusation.

"Oh, come, I've bagged the odd partridge," Wattle said.

"You were the finest marksman in your regiment."

"You exaggerate. I did my national service, everyone did in my day."

"You were known to be the best shot in the British Army of the Rhine." Schluessel was a military historian, but this degree of detail was remarkable. "In 1953, at the time of the coronation, your mess bet the French at Köln a case of champagne to drink the Queen's Toast. You beat Xavier de Villancourt in the final round."

"No, no," Wattle corrected him. "Xavo washed out in the semifinals. A chap from Mulhouse, an accountant in civilian life, I recollect, name of Bloch or Dreyfus or Durkheim or something like that, was the man I beat to win the bubbly."

Molly was sure Wattle was making this up and thought he'd rung just the right bell.

Schluessel also believed the last round to be a fabrication. "One of my ablest students is writing his dissertation on the British Army of the Rhine, and he says you beat Villancourt."

"I don't care what the meddling little prick told you." Wattle was no longer absentmindedly genial. "He has no business mucking about in the records of our mess."

Schuessel's students must be a far-flung lot; Molly expected he had protégés knowledgeable about each of the allied armies. Some working in London, some in Paris, some, almost certainly, in Washington. She wondered what Schluessel knew about Caleb Tuttle's war record. Perhaps that had been the subject of F. Barbarossa's research.

"Professor Wattle has surrendered his passport to me," the inspector said.

"I'm only a fellow actually." Wattle sounded modest, but any fellow of All Souls', Molly thought, would cherish that title above the most inflated alternative.

"Fellow Wattle has given me his passport." The inspector wanted a quieter life than was his at the moment. "I will explore your theory, Herr Doktor Professor Schluessel." He felt certain the German did not prefer understatement. "But I will not yet detain any persons on the basis of your most interesting suggestions."

"As you like. I will be at the lodge and at your service," Schluessel said and departed.

"I HADN'T REALIZED Schluessel saw you as such a Lorelei, my dear," Wattle said, after the police had withdrawn also. "I think sexual envy makes people far nastier than simple greed."

"He cannot be so filthy-minded as to believe the story he tells." Vorenchuk had risen when the police left the room and now paced, as Molly was accustomed to see virile persons pace, pounding his right fist into his left palm. "He shows his contempt for the Poles by relating it."

"He was provoking us." Molly agreed Schlussel's tale strained credulity. "He wants to find out how much we know."

"I think we should ourselves find out how much we know," Vorenchuk said. "Let me begin."

Molly remembered that he'd known, or supposed, that Healey was dead before she'd told him. Vorenchuk's story was simple. He'd gone to look for Bogdan Soltan after Healey had identified the priest as a Ukrainian. This information had not changed his views about the inadvisability of a trial, but he wanted to discuss the new development with Bogdan because he respected him. He could not find Bogdan and only this morning learned he was staying in Krakow. He'd spent almost an hour looking for him before concluding he was not to be found. "At that point, I decided to talk with Healey myself. No one at the conference was, to my knowledge, a supporter of Father Paul, but one never knows, and Schluessel had been around earlier, pressing upon me a most unpersuasive set of documents purporting to establish Paul as a Pole."

"Did you know where Healey was sleeping?" Molly wondered if she'd guessed right about his accomodations.

"No, but I know the palace. I found Healey easily, in a desirable suite, but I could not rouse him. There was a bottle of brandy by his bed and some prescription sleeping tablets."

"You don't think somebody'd explained his mistake and he'd taken enough to kill himself?" Wattle speculated that the whole ghastly show might have been staged to cover Healey's suicide.

"Healey seemed in no distress," Vorenchuk said. "I concluded he took a safe dose but would not be lucid before morning. His door locked automatically behind me and I thought him safe."

"Did you hear shots?" Molly asked. Vorenchuk related no difficulty entering Healey's room, but she'd had no trouble herself getting into Wolfi's.

"No. I later saw lights in the field, which gave me some disquiet but I thought many things might account for them."

"Did you hear anything?" she turned to Wattle.

"I may have. I heard some rat-ta-tat-tats and took them for firecrackers. It was midsummer's night. And a cry or two. I thought the traditional observances might account for those too."

The cry Molly had heard might, she supposed, have been sexual, but it hadn't struck her that way at the time. "Do you think the seminarian you were speaking with noticed anything unusual last night?"

"I'll ask him," Wattle said. He was returning to the palace and urging Molly to come with him, but she would not leave Wolfi. "If you're determined to remain here, my dear, I'll fetch some of your things."

Molly's skirt and sweater were muddy and blood-stained, and her hands, from which a nurse had removed many splinters, were wrapped in gauze. She preferred that Wolfi, who'd slept all afternoon, see nothing alarming in her appearance when he woke. "Would you?" Molly asked Wattle. "Clean clothes would be wonderful."

"Would you like me to stay with you?" Ivan Vorenchuk asked.

"I'd rather you found Bogdan Soltan," she told him. "He's with his cousin who's a filmmaker doing a life of Copernicus. He's called Petro. I'm not sure of his last name. He was in the United States with you last month."

Vorenchuk knew the man and the project. Petro Soltan—the fathers had been brothers—was filming at the Jagiellonian University and using its collection of astrological and scientific instruments, including Vorenchuk told her, a globe said to be the first to show the way to America.

"If you want to find it," she said.

"I have seen the new world to good advantage, today. Learning has not made you unwomanly." He kissed her bandaged hand. "Shall I now find Bogdan?"

"Please." Molly walked with him to the entrance of the hospital, where a crew of six men in crisply pressed Lufthansa overalls were unpacking, under the consul's energetic supervision, luggage vans holding enough equipment for a small field hospital.

IT WAS evening now. Wolfi had hardly stirred when the needles were inserted into his hands and arms, bearing the powerful medicines his powerful country had sent to save him. The consul had given Molly his card. "I'm putting my home telephone number on the back," he said. "The phones are reasonably dependable within the city. Call me at any hour. I have boundless respect for what Professor Ritter tries to do. Many of us have."

"I hope you will come back tomorrow and tell him that."

"Without fail."

Molly sat by Wolfi's bed thinking about his sorrows, wishing that some woman would love him in the ways she was unable to love him. And as she sat, wishing that, her mind was full of the fusing heat she recognized from the last stages of intellectual projects, when implicit notions were forged into theses and stray thoughts linked into causal chains.

CHAPTER

$$\boxed{26}$$

Bogdan Soltan did not like the boy's looks. In this, he may have agreed, for the first and only time in his life, with Helmut Schluessel. Nonetheless, Bogdan found Schluessel's tongue-lashing offensive.

"Charlie, you are an imbecile, a deracinated Slav more useless than the most backward peasant."

"I said I was sorry," Charlie said. "And I'm only half Ukrainian. Way back I betcha my family name was really 'Schmidt,' probably *von Schmidt.*'"

"*Von und zu Schmidt*, no doubt," Schluessel said cruelly and the boy did not catch his meaning; Charlie had no idea another prefix could add more prestige to "von." "*From* and *in* which smithy did your branch of the family arise? They must have been blacksmiths. They cannot have had the brains to be gunsmiths or the means to buy gold or silver."

"Oh, don't be so rough on the boy." Petro Soltan was lolling in a folding director's chair in the Renaissance courtyard of the Collegium Majus of the Jagiellonian University. His Copernicus pilot was complete and he was ready to start work on the epic. It was a beautiful June evening, and Petro was content.

"He is a cretin whose stupidity and indolence have jeopardized our enterprise." Charlie had given Schluessel some anxious moments the previous night.

Bogdan sat on a stone bench feeding the doves, whose soft grey feathers had been blackened by Krakow's sooty air, pleased to see Petro at odds with Schluessel. Their projected film was an embarrassment to him and the occasion, in Kiev and Lviv, of many bitter jokes. Petro invariably called their ridiculous movie a "joint venture" but everyone else used the older term, collaboration.

"Perhaps the grandfather smiths were locksmiths," Bogdan said, adding fuel to the fire. He thought the historian's own antecedents had not been exalted. "You and the professor may be distant cousins, young man. 'Schluessel' means 'key.' You may come from collateral branches of the same ancient family."

"Charlie's mistake did us no harm in the end." Petro was not displeased with the outcome. He believed great directors improvised: it had not occurred to him until he'd seen the Elector's palace that a prince of the church should give the mob general absolution. He'd puzzled for months over an artistic closure for the crowd scene.

"At least I didn't forget the friggin' lights," Charlie said, defending himself. "How can you have a friggin' screen test outdoors at night without no friggin' lights?"

"There was some mix-up last night?" Bogdan asked his cousin.

Petro yawned. "We were up half the night. I'd visualized a torch-lit execution of an evil moneylender. You know how effective night-time crowd scenes can be in black and white. And I am determined the entire film shall be shot in black and white, so the newsreels can be integrated more organically. That will be infinitely more authentic than colorizing the old clips. We went into the countryside to see about filming that sequence outdoors."

"And Baron von Schmidt," Schluessel said, "drove the

van to the wrong place. Tell me, Charlie, under what circumstances did your father reveal to you that your family name was 'Schmidt'?"

"He never said nothing. He's not really interested, but when I asked him, he said his folks came from England, way back. I guess on the *Mayflower* but before that they must have went from Germany to England."

"And at what period do you think your family migrated from Germany to England?" Schluessel asked.

He's a worse bully than he is a pedant, Bogdan thought, hoping yet to extricate his cousin Petro from this entanglement.

"Oh, before the war," Charlie said. "In the olden days, like in the eighteen hundreds. I think they like went to England on a Crusade and maybe even intermarried with the people there."

"And with what people did they intermarry?" Schluessel was a hateful man. "The Angles? the Jutes?"

"With the Wasps, I guess, yeah, most likely with the ancient Wasps."

"Charlie," Schluessel said. "You are the future and you make me sick. Nature and nurture have conspired to produce you to fill me with revulsion. In its integrated public schools the great colossus of the West has stuffed your Slavic cranium with dung."

"Kill them all," Bogdan said under his breath. He sat, unnoticed, as his father had sat while the enemy revealed its innermost thoughts and best-laid plans.

"Oh, yeah," Charlie said. "I ain't from California. I didn't go to school with no niggers. And I was smart enough to earn my castle. You're always talking about improvising, about commanders of genius laying their plans and then taking advantage of thuh unexpected." Charlie was an avid reader of *Soldier of Fortune*, and he'd taken to heart several of Schluessel's tactical maxims. "And don't forget"—Charlie was talking to Petro, rather

than to Schluessel—"don't you never forget I got you out
of a big jam when you forgot the truth serum."

"I am ever in your debt, Charlie," Petro Soltan said. "I
look forward to many boistrous revels in your ancestral
halls."

"Then you better get your ass in gear," Charlie said.
"The inside stuff, the plumbing and wiring, can wait till
winter, but you better get your guys cracking on the roof."

NONE OF them saw Bogdan get up from the bench and
leave the courtyard. He slipped out to join Ivan Vorenchuk, who beckoned to him from the gateway of the
Collegium Majus.

"So, the bilateral national epic is about to be filmed?"
Vorenchuk commiserated with his friend as they walked
along narrow streets towards the Planty, the ring of green
grass and trees that encircled Krakow's old city center.

"I fear I cannot stop Petro. I can't blame you for
avoiding him—and Helmut Schluessel. This film will be
a travesty."

"I've spent too much time with Schluessel already today," Vorenchuk said, pausing before a baroque church
of exceptional beauty and breathing a prayer. "Wolfgang
Ritter was badly wounded last night and the American
publicist Ignatius Healey was killed. Schluessel's taken a
great interest in the case."

"Will Ritter live?"

Vorenchuk said he didn't know.

"He is not the German who should be dying here. He's
a good man." Bogdan was thinking about Marta and about
Ritter's incomprehensible preference for the pretty American. She was sweet, but she was not, not Marta, simply
that. "I hope he makes it."

Vorenchuk thought there was much to be said for arranged marriages. These persons suffering in romantic

anarchy would be happier, he believed, if they'd been taught to live, in kindness and forbearance, with the mate bestowed upon them. He did not expect his views on this subject to prevail.

"Ritter had a gun apparently," Vorenchuk said.

"I was with him when he picked it up. He'd had words with Healey and Schluessel in Vienna and little Molly thought Healey had killed Caleb Tuttle."

"Healey himself condemned Father Paul last night in the hearing of many people who immediately grasped what he'd said. Ritter may have worked it out later."

Bogdan shrugged. "The priest's defenders will now have to produce an alibi. They'll say he was in Rustica. I've always expected it would come to that."

"Possibly. I looked for you for sometime afterward."

Bogdan said he'd rather sleep in a city than in a palace, and Ivan smiled. "I know you pride yourself on your proletarian origins, but Krakow's hardly a red town." They'd reached the Planty, the fine old park in which the citizens of Krakow had never ceased to saunter and to promenade: to be "anti- in the Planty" defined a polite skepticism about Marxist utopias.

"But Bogdan, seriously," Vorenchuk said. "Did Ritter confide in you what use he expected to make of the gun? Schluessel's telling the police Ritter shot Healey and then permitted an accomplice to wound him."

"Who's the accomplice? Does Schluessel know how well you shoot?"

"He's proposing Wattle."

"You're joking." After Vorenchuk assured him that he was not joking, Bogdan continued. "I've no idea what Ritter thought he'd do with a gun. Only, he thought that one person had already been killed to prevent Father Paul's trial, about which, my friend, I suppose we continue to disagree."

"We do," Vorenchuk said. "Let's take a tram to the

hospital." Municipal transit circled but did not encroach on the Planty, and they boarded a car for Nowa Huta. "Ritter may be conscious and the American woman is sensible. We should talk together." They did not resume their conversation until they got off the crowded tram at the hospital.

"Schluessel, I suppose," Vorenchuk asked, "understands nothing of any Slavic tongue?"

"He gets by with '*Achtung*' and '*schnell*.' But somebody could have explained the grammar to him," Bogdan said. He hoped that person had not been his cousin Petro. The two men had been working closely together.

MOLLY LOOKED out the window and then at her watch. Ten o'clock and still not dark. Wattle had come with her clothes and a touching story told him by the seminarian interested in fellow-feeling and natural sympathy. It was a remarkable tale, Wattle said, commemorated on a polychrome panel in the village church. She'd asked Wattle to substantiate the story as best he could, thanked him, kissed him, and sent him off. Now, washed and changed, she sat by Wolfi's bed, intent on puzzling out what had happened the previous night.

Wolfi had told her he'd seen Healey being carried off. But he would not have set off initially for Healey's room armed. That notion she'd recognized as absurd the moment she'd discovered the empty gun case under his bed. Wolfi must have gone to talk with Healey and found others had gotten there first. Why, then, had Wolfi not raised an alarm? Possibly, Molly speculated, because Healey had not seemed to be in immediate danger.

Possibly Wolfi thought Healey was being spirited out of danger? He hadn't been shouting for help or others would have heard him too. She and Wolfi had seen him take a bottle of brandy from the terrace and Vorenchuk confirmed he'd had pills too. Suppose Healey appeared too drunk or dopey to walk and friends were helping him, friends like Schluessel, for example.

Wolfi decided to follow them, but had gone first for his rifle, to protect himself against Schluessel—who was staying at a hunting lodge with access to guns—and to defend Healey should the abduction not be well intended. One did not know whether Schluessel wanted to keep him safe or keep him quiet. Healey had, Molly believed, really thought Father Paul a victim of mistaken identity, and it was one thing to accept genocide as providential and quite another to defend a man who'd personally killed hundreds of people. Healey might or might not shrink from that. Schluessel, contemptuous of Americans, might well expect that he would shrink from that. So Wolfi followed them.

This scenario, Molly thought, got Wolfi and his gun plausibly into the fields beyond the palace garden, though probably he had not gone through the garden. She'd seen nothing moving there; and he'd questioned her fairly closely, considering that he was barely conscious, about crossing the brook and coming up its steep bank. Maybe that *had* been dangerous. She hadn't walked into a firefight, but, in retrospect, she realized no infantryman would have gone about it the way she had. Wolfi had probably doubled around by the road and approached the field more intelligently.

The question remained. How many people were willing to kill to protect Father Paul? If Healey had killed Tuttle, had another supporter of the priest come forward to dispatch him? Or had Healey cooperated in the first murder with others prepared now to sacrifice him too? And what role in any of this belonged to Charlie Smith, who'd seemed to be measuring his castle for aluminum siding—

a ruined castle outside Lviv for which the Ukrainian Ministry of Culture cherished more ambitious plans?

The room was getting darker: electrical lights were not
used unnecessarily. The surgeon had come half an hour
before to check on Wolfi. They'd talked for a while: the
doctor was able to tell her only that Wolfi was no worse—
he'd hoped to see more improvement, she sensed, and did
not want to leave abruptly, as if he'd lost hope. He spoke
beautiful French and Molly'd asked him where he'd studied before Paris. He told her that he'd lived his entire life
in Krakow but that his mother and his grandmother were
old pupils of Sacred Heart schools. Molly had not been
surprised, and she was grateful for his upbringing as she
lit the kerosene lamp he'd left for her.

"You are really here, aren't you?" Wolfi said.

"Yes, and you are really awake and well."

"Awake," he said. "Are we in Poland?" The room did
look, apart from its dim and flickering light, like a show-
room for top-of-the-line hospital supplies.

"The German consul in Krakow had all this sent, because of his regard for you."

"Efficient."

"More than that, Wolfi, much more than that. I'd like
the doctor to know you're awake."

"Stay for a moment," he said, and she recognized he
was quoting Goethe, "you are so lovely."

THE PHYSICIAN would not hear of any visitors for Pan
Ritter tonight. Thank the most merciful Lord that he was
conscious, and Miss Rafferty could, of course, remain
with him. But no other person. Absolutely not.

Ivan Vorenchuk and Bogdan Soltan said they would
wait until Ritter slept again to speak with her: Vorenchuk
went to the hospital's newly completed chapel and Bog-

dan to its cafeteria, which had not been painted since 1971. The cold food, however, was more plentiful and various than in Ukraine and he ate a hearty meal. When he finished he took a cup of powdered coffee to Molly and, after she drank it, they went to talk with Vorenchuk in the handsome modernist chapel.

"How many people heard Healey last night?" Bogdan asked. He had left the palace while Healey was still talking about a three-chambered parliament.

"I did. Schluessel, several of the seminarians, including one who later had a long talk with Wattle, Molly and Ritter," Ivan Vorenchuk said. "Any number of people may have been in the garden within earshot."

"My cousin Petro was in the garden late that night," Bogdan said. "He had a brainstorm about putting the palace into his disgusting film. His helper took a wrong turn, and he decided to throw in a bishop giving the bloodthirsty mob absolution after they impale the moneylender."

"Impale the moneylender?"

Molly had leapt to her feet and Vorenchuk asked more calmly, "How do they impale him? Pitchfork or stake?"

"Haypole. It's more effective, silhouetted against the sky, or so Petro says."

"You do know that's how I found Healey?" Molly asked.

"You said he'd been shot," Bogdan said. "You said Schluessel told the police Ritter shot him."

"He'd been shot, too," Molly said.

Bogdan was silent for some minutes. "It cannot be coincidence. I was surprised Schluessel seemed so interested in rural ways."

"Did Petro know Healey?" Ivan Vorenchuk asked this question evenly, in no leading manner.

"He never mentioned him."

"I believe Healey did not know him, but expected to meet him. I found this among the papers in Healey's room last night." Vorenchuk took from his passport case a glossy print of the Ukrainian delegation seated around Caleb Tuttle's dinner table, folded in half and in half again. He unfolded it and taped across the top was the transparent diagram Molly had tried so hard to memorize. "Healey was in no state to preserve discretion. I thought it would be better for us and for him, if it were in a safer place."

"I saw the photograph in Boston," Molly said. "And the diagram was mailed to Healey from Austria. At least I saw it on the plane in an envelope mailed from Austria with a paper for the conference. I'd never heard of the author and no scholar of that name came to the conference."

"What do you think it means?" Vorenchuk asked her, "I thought it was a key to your delegation. Members were more than, less than, or equal to something. Marta and you, Ivan, were less than something. Bogdan and Kyril Dobrylko were equal . . . I'm not sure."

"Has anybody tried to contact Marta?" Bogdan asked. He had not yet taken that step but he knew where duty lay.

Molly had thought about it, but she'd been unwilling to leave Wolfi for the length of time she thought it would take to call Yalta, assuming it were possible to call Yalta.

"I sent a telegram," Ivan said.

"You omit no good deed," Bogdan said, turning his attention again to the photograph. "My cousin Petro is more than whatever it is. What do you make of it?"

"From the point of view of Healey or Healey's correspondent? More than one would expect." Vorenchuk suggested.

More cooperative, Molly thought, more sympathetic.

And she thought those assessments were accurate. Ivan Vorenchuk believed Father Paul should not be brought to trial, but he'd not touch Schluessel's forgeries. Marta was sophisticated and lively: she'd entertain any idea, listen to any argument, but principle and sentiment made her immovable on this issue. Bogdan was what he appeared to be, a tough-minded patriot with scores to settle. Kyril Dobrylko, too, was easy to read: he went out on no limbs and if he did he landed on his feet. Petro, on the other hand, might appear a weak reed, but he was more promising than he looked.

"I must talk to Petro," Bogdan said.

CHAPTER

27

MOLLY WAS lying down in the nurses' dormitory, a cool, dark room with cots set close together. Every other woman in the room, she thought, was sleeping the deep, disciplined sleep of those who work to the point of exhaustion and must be up shortly to work again. Ivan Vorenchuk had insisted on taking her place beside Ritter. The doctor had told her what he'd said: that she was a heroic woman but she'd been awake for forty hours. Sleep would refresh her spirit as well as her body, and he agreed with Vorenchuk's prescription. The patient was rather better; he would send for her, he promised, if there were any change.

Molly had hesitated, with the mad thought that reactionaries, however chivalrous, might let Wolfi die. No, she thought, Vorenchuk and this Polish doctor are good men. My fear is delusional and I had better get some sleep. She was grateful to be stretched out on cold linen, a small flat pillow rough beneath her cheek. Ignatius Healey impaled, she was reflecting on that. Ignatius Healey, with or without silk pajamas, executed as oppressors, or supposed oppressors, had once been. The brainstorm of a flake quick to improvise.

Improvisation. That was it. Schluessel had not set out to kill Wolfi; he'd seized an opportunity to kill or disgrace him and he was indifferent which of those two ends he achieved. Either one was more than he'd hoped for. Wolfi, armed and rushing to Healey's defense—no, not rushing, advancing according to some intelligent plan—Wolfi's valor offered Schluessel an opportunity to destroy both men. How, then, had Schluessel managed to shoot Wolfi if he'd been advancing cautiously in a field that provided plenty of cover?

She wasn't sure, but she was fairly confident she had the outlines of the story right. Wolfi had been shot first, and cried out in surprise as much as in pain. He'd dropped his rifle and others had used it to shoot away Healey's face. There had been no human sound after the second shots because Healey had already bled to death before they were fired. That settled, she slept until morning.

"YES, BOGDAN, yes, I did it. Stop it, Bogdan," Petro Soltan was terrified that his cousin would stop shaking him and begin beating him. "I went back to Tuttle's house the morning I missed the train to New York." Bogdan had taken the tram to the Krakow apartment they'd been sharing, lent to Petro by a musician friend performing abroad, and hauled his cousin out of bed.

"Yeah, Petro's a fuck-up." Their shouting had roused Charlie Smith who'd been rolled up in a blanket on the floor. The boy stood up, scrawny and dirty, in jockey shorts that had not been laundered for many days. "You can't depend on him for nothing. He even forgot the truth serum he was supposed to bring for Caleb Tuttle."

"Get dressed both of you and come with me," Bogdan thundered. "Schluessel kills people who are no longer useful to him."

"No way," Charlie said. "We're going back to Lemberg today to start the renovations on my castle."

"What castle is this?"

Charlie blurted out all his dreams: the castle; the film career, and, if he tired of acting, a commission in the army or a command in the Black Sea fleet; the many beautiful princesses who had been in exile ever since Churchill who was crazy and Roosevelt who was a Jew met with Gorbachev at Yalta.

Bogdan destroyed that vision, brutally, though the boy was so ignorant Bogdan found it difficult to explain why his wishes could not be easily granted. When he explained the castle belonged to the Ministry of Culture, Charlie offered to let the culture guys use it a couple times a year. When he explained that decent people were hoping to eliminate political favoritism in the army, Charlie thought the duke, his father-in-law, could tell the generals, like, to shove it. They'd have to take him and promote him. Gulling Charlie Smith, Bogdan thought, must have taken less time than setting him straight. At last, Charlie appeared convinced his plans had suffered a temporary check. He found his shirt and jeans and went with the cousins to the hospital.

MOLLY AND Ivan Vorenchuk were waiting for them in the hospital cafeteria, and in that stark room, Charlie Smith told his tale. A man had called him some months ago and told him he'd been chosen for a special mission. Everything was on a need-to-know basis. He had to find out some things about Caleb Tuttle, what he did during the day, what he liked to eat and drink. He'd carried out that reconnaissance so well that he'd been given a more difficult task. He was to rendezvous with a courier bringing truth serum to stop Caleb Tuttle from telling lies about the war. The caller was a German; the courier would be a Ukrainian. The mission was to be the work of a unified strike force.

Charlie's eyes narrowed, cunningly. "I knew it wasn't no truth serum. They all wear off. There's only one kinda drink shuts you up for good. Petro forgot the stuff he was supposed to bring, so I used the Bug-Off me and Jimmy hid in the cellar."

"And after you murdered a man who saved the lives of most of your relatives . . ." Bogdan's father had known Tuttle, though even Tuttle had not known the part he played. "What then?"

"I came over here. For my screen test. I wasn't sure I'd get the castle, but I learned my lines."

This level of moral idiocy would have been unbelievable had not Petro seconded the boy. "You know what art will be like, after your velvet revolutions," the filmmaker said angrily. "No more subsidized theatre companies. No more *Boris Gudunov* in the soccer stadium. It'll be every man for himself. The thieving Croatians had this deal almost nailed down."

"And what happened, Charlie, the night before last?" Molly asked.

"Oh, jeez, I had to drive the van with all the props, the dummy I was gonna put on the haypole and the weapons and all the frigging equipment to the place where I was gonna have my screen test but I ended up at this palace."

"That turned out well, actually," Petro said, and Bogdan raised his hand as if to strike him, then slapped the cafeteria table instead.

"Did it?" Bogdan said. "Tell us."

"It might have turned out better than it did," Petro acknowledged. He was afraid of his cousin and seemed unable at this point to tell him anything but the truth. "I was going back and forth between the fields and the palace grounds plotting out a scene and I ran into Schluessel, who told me that Healey had made some tremendous gaffe but he wasn't sure what it was. We decided to hustle him out and Schluessel told Charlie to move the car to a more secluded spot and wait for us."

The cafeteria was filling up now: shifts were changing and people who'd worked for twenty-four hours drank weak tea, too exhausted to eat. Others were eating, methodically, before their day began. None paid any attention to the people who lowered their voices to continue discussing the events of midsummer's night.

"Schluessel told me to move the van down a dirt road and pull in, into a little lane, like. I was supposed to fire a warning shot if I seen anybody coming along the road."

"There were guns among your theatrical props?" Ivan Vorenchuk asked.

"Yeah, real ones. Schluessel brought them from the hunting lodge. He told me to fire into the air if I seen anybody. He was real nasty about how he thought I could hit the air. But I seen this guy coming down the road with a gun so I plugged him. Schluessel had a cow when he saw the guy lying in the road. But he calmed down when he turned him over and said maybe things would be all right."

"You helped Schluessel carry the man you'd shot into the hayfield? Yes?" Vorenchuk continued his questioning. "And then?"

"Then I had my screen test, actually it was more like a rehearsal. After I save the girl, I kill the bad guy and stick him up on a pole. I'd left the dummy in the car and Schluessel said I could use a real body instead."

"A live body?" Molly would not have expected this even of Schluessel.

"They told me he'd committed suicide. And it

wouldn't, like hurt his family's feelings so much if they thought he'd been murdered."

"Did his body feel dead to you?" Ivan Vorenchuk had never touched a corpse without reverence for its departed soul.

"I don't know," Charlie said. "He felt pretty limp. Sure, yeah, he was dead. How should I know?"

"Charlie, did you shoot him with the other man's gun, after you got him up on the pole?" Molly asked this.

"No, Schluessel did. He said he didn't want anything to go wrong."

Charlie's tale revealed depths of ignorance and credulity Molly would not have thought possible. She feared his tempters had secured for themselves total deniability. Soon she would have to educate him about plea bargaining.

GERVASE WATTLE and the robust seminarian came to see Molly later in the day with a simpler and more beautiful story. They had talked in the Elector's garden about Adam Smith's moral psychology. The youth agreed that people often felt compassion spontaneously and without reflection; many times, too, shared symbols helped them recognize their common feelings. He'd illustrated his point with a legend from his native village, Rustica, and invited Wattle to come with him to see the painting that commemorated the event.

Wattle had been unable to do that yesterday because they'd been looking after Wolfi, but they'd gone early this morning. Wattle had been moved by what he saw and he made some notes which he gave to Molly. She called the German consul, who agreed to check them out. The records from that period were not computerized, he informed her, but he was certain they'd been preserved.

* * *

"WOLFI," MOLLY said, "I know where your father was on the Feast of the Assumption in 1942."

Such pain as she'd given him since he'd first met her had been beyond her power to assuage and he expected only kindness from her now. "You know and it makes no difference?"

"It will make a difference to you. Your father was not at Zborodny. Physical evidence places him at a village called Rustica. The story is so famous in the region that people expect Father Paul will claim to have been there too. But your father was definitely there."

And she told him about the winds that blew out the candles lit before the shrine of the Blessed Mother. The villagers lit them again and again, and the wind extinguished them. A prosperous farmer had brought light bulbs from the city, but they had no power to illuminate them until a German officer appeared, a knightly stranger, and connected them to the battery of his beautiful car.

"My father cannot have been the only German officer willing to do that."

"The seminarian, Stanislas, says the man was called Colonel Ritter."

"Molly, that sounds too much like the kind of emblematic naming one gets in folk tales."

"You are a meticulous scholar," she said. "Try this. Wattle has seen a painting that captures the magic of the event as experienced by rural people unaccustomed to electricity. The incandescent wires, he says, glow inside the clear light bulbs like stamens in a flower and the night is as day. You can read the license plate on the Mercedes."

"It would be possible to verify that, naturally." Wolfi knew what to expect of army archives.

"The consul had the numbers verified in a matter of hours."

"I wonder if my father's superiors sent him there," he said. "So he would not disgrace himself by insubordination and put an end to his usefulness to them."

"Possibly," she said. "In any event, he was not at Zborodny during the massacre."

Tears flowed down his cheeks, and because his hands and arms were still immobilized with medical apparatus, Molly wiped them away. "The consul will be coming to see you," she said. "He's so prompt and zealous I can't think what's kept him."

"It would not be so bad, Molly, if he was late," Wolfi said. And they had a hour or so alone together.

AN INCIDENT at the German frontier had occupied his day, the consul explained when he arrived, joyful to see Professor Ritter looking so well. Problems had arisen with the documents of a nun, a deaf-mute she seemed at first, trying to cross the border in a rented car. The police had attempted to help the good sister but she was uncooperative, struck one of them and tried to flee, and in the ensuing scuffle her habit became disarranged. Impersonating a nun might be a gross indecency rather than a crime, the Polish officials had explained, apologetically, when they called him; but Herr Doktor Professor Schluessel was wanted for questioning in another matter and he was demanding they send for the nearest German consul.

"I went immediately, naturally, and found Schluessel, still in his nun's habit, in a small police barracks. He was raving about Panzer divisions crossing the frontier in '39. He said Germans could still move in that direction like a hot knife through their filthy rancid butter. If they would not let him go in the other direction he would kill them all. I was aghast. I have worked in Poland for five long years trying to build trust. Some of the Poles were embarrassed for me, I think."

"I'm sure you've made many friends here," Molly said. This man, though not unduly self-conscious, was as good as gold.

"Schluessel was so, so beyond reason. He kept tripping over his long black skirts and the stuffing in his bosom fell out and his beard was growing through his face powder, and I thought, involuntarily, about all the Weimar cross-dressers and how Hermann Goering was said to paint his face. I started to laugh. I could not help myself."

Wolfi himself was laughing, quietly at first and then as unreservedly as his bandages and intravenous drips would permit. "How did you recover from this breach of decorum?" Wolfi asked. Molly had not seen him laugh since she'd arrived in Vienna.

"We were all laughing together, the Poles and I, quite helplessly, until Schluessel tried to escape and I knocked him down. One of them said, 'Let's shoot him, he's trying to escape.' But I could not permit the joke to go that far."

"And after this wonderful, fraternal moment?" Molly asked.

"We discussed our positions. The Poles, as we know, do not detain foreigners wanted for questioning. They simply hold their passports. They said they could not extend this courtesy to a person who'd already tried to exit in an illicit manner. They would have to incarcerate the gentleman. I told them I would do the same in their place."

"Schluessel's going to jail," Molly almost shouted in triumph, "in Poland?"

"For some time, I expect," the consul said. "There's a considerable increase in the crime rate, with the greater degree of freedom, and the courts are backlogged." The Poles and the Americans would have many months to negotiate the manner in which Schluessel and Charlie Smith and Petro Soltan would be put on trial.

A nurse came with a message for Molly. "I have to go out for a while, Wolfi," she said. "Cardinal Hollihan is clamoring for news of you and I've been summoned to call him on the archbishop's reliable telephone."

"You should call Nick, too," he said. "If word of this has reached America, he may have heard of it. He will be worried about you."

AFTER JOHN, Cardinal Hollihan, heard Molly's account of the events and thanked heaven Ritter would recover, he handed the phone to Nick.

"Stay, babe," Nick told her, after listening to her story, "as long as you think you should." Nick did not imagine he loved her more than Wolfgang Ritter did, but he did not love her any less. "As long as you want." Maybe she'd need some time, maybe she had feelings for Ritter she hadn't felt before.

"I won't stay much longer," she said. "Nick, anything your mother wants to do about the wedding is all right with me. I just want to marry you."

"Are you sure?"

"Yes."

"Are you sure?" he asked again and this time she understood what he was asking. She told him Wolfi was dear to her, yes, they were closer than they'd ever been; but he was the man she wanted to marry, as soon as the ceremony could be arranged.

"This cover-up has already killed two men and nearly killed Ritter. That's enough for me." John, Cardinal Hollihan, said, pressing a button on the speakerphone he used for less sensitive matters. "Timmy, get me the Secretary of State."

There was no answer but the sound of thudding foot-

steps, and Tim Lynch rushed into the low-ceilinged parlor. Nick Hannibal had hung up the other phone and
stood, looking out at the honeysuckle, breathing deeply.
The cardinal stood behind his desk.

"Your Eminence," Father Lynch said. "You can't."

"Can't what?"

"Can't send a priest back into captivity. There may be
another coup. They'll execute him no matter who's in
power."

"Where is God, Timmy?"

"What?"

"Where is God?" the cardinal thundered.

Timothy Lynch was dumfounded. The cardinal was
supposed to have a temper; there were legends about his
towering rages, mostly in connection with mortgage fore-
closures and accidents in the mines.

"Father Lynch, have you forgotten your catechism?
'Where is God?'"

"Everywhere, Your Eminence," Timothy Lynch stam-
mered. "God is everywhere."

"Then He will hear an act of contrition made in Kiev."